I0745308

VALKYRIE

COVEN: BOOK 3

DAVID NETH

DN Publishing

Valkyrie
Coven, Book 3
Copyright © 2021 by David Neth
Batavia, NY

www.DavidNethBooks.com

ISBN: 978-1-945336-12-6
First Edition

Subscribe to the author's newsletter for updates and exclusive content:
DavidNethBooks.com/Newsletter

Follow the author at:
www.facebook.com/DavidNethBooks

Also by David Neth

<u>Coven</u>
Harpy
Siren
Valkyrie
Shapeshifter
Sorcerer
Enchantress
Oracle

<u>Under the Moon</u>
The Full Moon
The Harvest Moon
The Blood Moon
The Crescent Moon
The Blue Moon

The Art of Magic

<u>Fuse</u>
Origin
Omertá
Oblivion

<u>Heat</u>
Black Magnet
Dust Storm
The Gatekeeper

<u>Standalone</u>
All I Ever Wanted

CHAPTER 1

– AUGUST 1988 –

I realize helping me set up our romantic date isn't exactly romantic." Samantha grabbed two corners of the green tablecloth with a glittering floral pattern weaved in with a darker shade of green.

Steven grabbed the opposite two corners and helped fan it out over the table. "Who says perfection is romance?" With the tablecloth now covering the table, Steven ambled to Samantha and hooked his arm around her while she straightened it out. "I have you, a delicious meal, and the house to ourselves."

Heels clunked on the hardwood, as if on cue. Moments later, Kathy came down the stairs in a tight red dress.

"You'll be by yourselves in two minutes." She pulled at the hem to cover up more of her legs, then dug through her clutch.

"I'm going downtown again tonight. I'll be home late, so don't wait up."

Samantha stared wide-eyed at her sister. "Kathy, you look—"

"Amazing, I know." Kathy smiled and then moved to the mirror in the foyer and applied her lipstick.

"I mean, it's a little revealing," Samantha said. "Are you even comfortable? You look like you're going to pop out."

Kathy hooked an eyebrow and looked at her sister and Steven. "Are you calling me fat?"

Steven turned away quickly and disappeared into the kitchen.

Samantha rolled her eyes. Kathy ran every morning, unless she was doing kickboxing or some other physical exercise. Fat was the last word anyone would use to describe her and even Kathy knew it.

"I just want you to be careful," Samantha said. "You and I both know all of the weirdos that are out and about."

"Okay, *Mom*." Kathy finished applying her lipstick, closed the tube, and slipped it back in her clutch.

"Who are you going with again?" Samantha asked.

Trisha.

"Is that who you've been going out with the last few weeks?" Samantha asked.

Kathy looked up at her sister. "I didn't give you a name yet."

Samantha looked confused. "You didn't? I thought I heard—"

"You must be hearing things," Kathy said. "I'm going with Trisha."

"That's what I thought you said!"

Kathy gave her sister a confused look. "*Anyway*, like I *did* say, don't wait up for me."

"Are you taking my car?"

"No, I called a cab," Kathy said. "It should be here any minute."

Samantha nodded and continued to set the table, laying out the candles and the plate settings. Ever since Kathy and Jeremy had broken up, she'd been going out to a bar or a club—or both—every weekend with Trisha. As much as Samantha liked her sister doing what she wanted without the worry of Jeremy to control her, she was concerned her sister was having a bit *too much* fun.

Kathy's heels clonked on the hardwood as she walked over to the table. "Fancy dinner?"

"Kind of an important one," Samantha murmured. "Tonight's the night."

The younger sister raised her eyebrows. "Are you ready?"

"As ready and I'll ever be."

"Do you want me to stay home?"

As much as Samantha liked the idea of Kathy actually having a night in—and a Thursday night at that, something

Kathy referred to as "Thirsty Thursday"—Samantha knew she couldn't control her sister. And it would be better if she wasn't home.

"No, you go and have fun," Samantha said.

From the street, a car honked twice.

"That must be my cab," Kathy said. "Are you sure you'll be okay?"

"I'll be fine. Now go."

"Good luck," she called as she walked to the door.

Samantha yelled to her sister, "Be careful!"

As she finished setting the table, Steven came in with their food, steaming from just coming off the stove.

"That smells delicious," she said.

"Well, you did most of the work." He set the dishes on the table. "So pat yourself on the back."

"Ugh, you know my arm gets tired from doing that all the time." She smirked and allowed him to pull out her chair for her.

"Did your sister leave?" He came around the opposite side of the table and took his own seat.

"Yeah."

Good, she heard in his voice, but she didn't see his lips move so she didn't say anything.

"She's been out a lot lately," he said. "Not that I'm complaining. It gives us more time together." He reached across the table and squeezed her hand before dishing out their plates.

"She has," Samantha admitted. "I think it's still an after-effect of her breakup with Jeremy. Her way of coping with it."

Jeremy and Kathy didn't have a great relationship, she heard in Steven's voice. "Who is she even going out with?" he asked out loud.

She stared at him, confused at what was going on, but snapped out of it. This was probably just nerves about what she needed to tell him. What she tried to tell him several times but had been cut off or distracted. Tonight, she wasn't going to put up with anymore excuses.

Of course, she had said that before, too.

"Uh, Trisha," Samantha said.

Who the hell is Trisha?

"She was in Kathy's grade in high school," Samantha responded. "They were friends, not close, but they knew each other. Fell out of touch after high school and reconnected at a club."

Probably not the best influence for Kathy. "Gotcha," he said. "So an old friend?"

She narrowed her eyes, but relaxed her face when he finished dishing out their plates. "Yeah."

"Well, not to shift the subject off of your sister," he started, "but I've been doing some number crunching."

An image of a ranch-style house with a flower garden out front and a manicured lawn popped into Samantha's head. *He wants to buy a house*, she thought.

"I added up my income with yours and calculated how

much the two of us would qualify for a mortgage," he said.

"Steven, we're not even married yet," she said.

"So? We can buy the house anytime and have it ready for when we are married." *Maybe move in ahead of time and get away from your sister.*

"I'm not ready to move yet," she said. "I like it here. And we haven't even set a date for the wedding yet."

"I thought we were looking at January?"

"Yeah, but we still have to decide where we're doing it, settle on a guest list, figure out what we're going to feed people, and, oh yeah, pick the actual date!"

"We can get to that," he said. "But having a place to live is important too." *Typical girl, only thinking about the wedding.*

Samantha raised her hands to her forehead. "You know what? I can't talk about this right now."

You never want to talk about this. Steven looked down at his meal and stabbed it with his fork with more force than he needed. *We're going to be living with Kathy for the rest of our lives. Sexless marriage, here we come!*

"I have something else to tell you," she said.

A baby?

"No, it's not a baby," she said quickly.

"I didn't say anything about a baby," he replied.

She got a little red in the face, her heart thumping against her chest.

"Honey, your hand's shaking." He reached across the table

to take one of hers in both of his. "What's going on?" *Cancer? Is she sick? Is that why she doesn't want to commit to buying a house?*

She swallowed to try to moisten her dry throat, but it didn't work. "I'm a witch."

CHAPTER 2

Tommy Wilson crossed West 5th Street, where he parked in the lot just off Peach Street, and went in the back entrance to The 814 nightclub. Named after Erie's phone number area code, it was one of the few nightclubs in the city.

It was the last place he wanted to be after a full shift with the Erie Police Department, but it's what he needed to do to support his family. And the club was the only job that allowed him the flexibility to work around his police schedule. Plus, they liked it that he was also a police officer.

Inside, the manager and two of the bartenders were hauling cases of drinks from the cooler to the bar. Once the crowd filled in, there'd be no hope of getting through easily with a case of drinks like this. Better to be fully stocked from the beginning of the night. Tommy knew. He used to be a bartender back in college.

"Jared, how's it going?" he called out.

The manager set his case on the bar and stepped over to shake Tommy's hand. "I'm hanging in there. Glad you could come in tonight."

"No problem," he said. "Need any help with anything?"

Jared turned back to the bar where the bartender was putting the drinks away. "Nah, we've got it covered. My other bartenders should be here soon." He checked his watch.

"Anything I need to be aware of tonight?" Tommy made it a habit of checking in with Jared before his shift started. Thursday nights were when the weekend crowd started to ramp up and with the summer heat still looming over the city, people were quick to jump to hostility. Especially when they'd been drinking.

"Actually, yeah. Follow me." Jared started walking off to the hallway at the back, past the bathrooms, and through the small kitchen. They stepped into the small office and Jared grabbed a printout of a black and white security camera image. The photo was grainy, but Tommy recognized the man as a regular.

"He giving you problems?"

"Yeah, this guy's bad news," Jared said. "Tuesday night and Wednesday night—our slow nights—he got a little friendly with some of the girls. Inside security told him to stop, but he didn't."

"Of course." Tommy studied the picture some more.

"At one point, he even tried to lure a girl into the bathroom, where there's obviously no camera," Jared went on. "Louie, who was working that night—last night, I think—kicked him out. Noticed afterward that the girl he was talking to was really out of it. We think he might've spiked her drink. We got her a cab and sent her home."

"Drugs, man," Tommy said.

"Lovely little things, aren't they? Anyway, Louie told this guy he wasn't welcome back and I agree completely. Haven't heard from the girl, so I don't know if she's pressing charges or anything. He's just lucky you weren't working that night or he would've been arrested."

Should've been, Tommy thought. *The police station is right across the park and this guy still tried to pull something like this.*

"You got a name for him?" Tommy asked.

"Eugene Richards, according to his ID," Jared said. "I guess his friends call him Dickie."

"Cute."

"Can't expect a lot of ingenuity out of these guys," Jared said. "Other than him, that's all I've got for you."

Tommy handed back the picture. "Hopefully it'll be a quiet night, but I'll keep an eye out for him."

"If he gives you any trouble at the door, just flag one of the inside guys down," Jared said. "I'm not messing around with drugging girls' drinks. That's not the type of club we have here."

"I can handle this guy." Tommy turned to step out of the

office with Jared in tow. "I handle much worse on a daily basis."

"I'm sure you do." Jared patted Tommy on the back. "I wouldn't want your job."

Tommy laughed. "Most people don't. I'm going to head out and start putting up the line queues before the crowd starts. They should be showing up anytime now."

"Sounds good, Tommy," Jared said. "Be careful out there."

"I always am."

CHAPTER 3

"A witch?" Steven gave Samantha a suspicious look. *How much wine has she had to drink? Did I even bring any wine out? Has she been drinking in her bedroom?*

"I'm not a drunk," she said.

"I didn't say you were." He looked at her with even more concern, before his expression turned lighter, the corners of his mouth turning up in a smile. "A witch? You're really bad at jokes sometimes." Steven pulled away and returned to his food.

"This isn't a joke," she said. "Think about all of the unexplained absences I've had over the years. The canceled dates, the forced living arrangements last month."

Steven stared at her, fork raised. He didn't say a word, but she could still hear his voice: *This is insane. A witch? She does act really strange sometimes. And there have been a lot of unanswered questions. But a witch? They're not real. Are they?*

"You're serious," he finally said.

She nodded and reached over and grabbed a flower from the vase in the center of the table.

Release the strength of my power,
To speed the life of this flower.

In an instant, the petals stretched further before wilting and turning brown.

Steven jumped back in his seat. He looked at her, trying to get a better read on her by looking in her eyes. *Is she going to hex me if I don't react the way she wants? What way am I supposed to react? Is this why she didn't want to get married in a church? Is it because she worships the devil?*

"No devil worship here," she said quickly. "Kathy and I are good witches."

"I didn't say—Kathy's a witch too?"

"Well, yeah," Samantha said with the hint of a smirk. "She's my sister. Of course she is. But listen, I'm trusting you with this because I love you. You can't tell *anyone* that Kathy and I are witches. It could…it could be really bad."

Was she not going to tell me if we weren't getting married? "So you've been lying to me all this time?" Steven got to his feet.

"Not because I wanted to." Samantha jumped up too and

came around the table. She reached for him, but he pushed her away. "I had to. For your own protection. But if we're going to be husband and wife, we can't keep secrets from each other."

"I thought we made that promise to each other a long time ago?" he asked. "Remember? You told me that I knew everything there was to know about you?"

She gulped. "I did, but—"

"But were you just lying? Just telling me what I wanted to hear? Were you ever going to tell me this if I didn't propose?"

Samantha didn't have an answer for him because she didn't know if she would have. If he didn't propose, what would be the tipping point for her telling him her secret? Would it be a threat against his life? He had been targeted by supernatural forces before. What if one finally got him and the last thing he heard before he died—the last thing he *felt*—was how the woman he loved betrayed him by keeping a secret. In that sense, Steven proposing to her forced her hand and maybe even saved his life.

Tears pooled in Samantha's eyes as she considered the possibilities and consequences of what could've happened if she had continued to keep this secret all to herself.

Steven looked at her, the pain evident on his face. "I guess I can take that as a no."

"I'm so sorry," she muttered around the lump in her throat. "I should've told you sooner."

Would she have?

"I wish I did!"

Does she really love me? Does she even know what that means?

"Steven, I love you so much." She stepped to him and reached for his hand, but he pulled away.

"I need to go." His voice was emotionless, although it was evident in his cold look what he was feeling. He turned and started for the door. *Maybe there won't be a wedding after all.*

"No!" She started following him. "We don't need to cancel the wedding! Let's just think this over."

Steven turned and looked at her. "What is this? You're a witch and suddenly you can read minds?"

Stopping in her tracks, Samantha absently played with her engagement ring. *Could* she read minds? Was that what she'd been picking up on lately? All the extra voices she'd been hearing?

"I don't—"

"Well, get out of mine!" He slammed the door behind him as he left.

CHAPTER 4

The line outside The 814 had dwindled to nothing as the evening turned into the early morning hours. Tommy allowed himself a small reprieve from watching the door to take down the line queues along the sidewalk. From inside, the music thumped and the chatter of a crowd could be heard over it all.

Thursday nights were certainly busier than Wednesday nights, but not as crowded as Fridays or especially Saturdays. These weekday shifts were Tommy's favorite because they were easy shifts. Fridays and Saturdays there were always a few people who wanted to make a name for themselves or just go out to cause trouble.

Tommy lit a cigarette and paced up and down the sidewalk

in front of the club, keeping an eye out for anything he would need to step in to stop. Other than the music from the club and some chatter from bars further down North Park Row, downtown Erie was pretty quiet.

As he turned back to return to his post by the door, Tommy caught sight of the man he'd been keeping an eye out for all night: Dickie. Dressed to impress in his ripped jeans and sleeveless flannel to show off the tattoos up and down his arms, Dickie walked up to Tommy confidently.

"What's the cover, my man?" he asked.

"Well, for everyone inside, there was no cover tonight," Tommy said. "For you, I was told to keep you out here."

Dickie got angry. "By who?"

Tommy waved the hand holding his cigarette between his fingers. "Doesn't matter who. Those are the rules."

"Give me their name!" He got close to Tommy's face. A form of intimidation he had seen many times before as a police officer and one that he had grown immune to.

"Take a step back and let's talk about this, okay?"

Dickie slowly stepped away and looked Tommy up and down. "One of those girls rat me out?"

"Is there something you need to be ratted out about?" Tommy asked. Since he wasn't in uniform, he decided he wasn't going to hold back this time.

No response.

"Look, let's examine some of the facts, shall we?" Tommy

started. "If I let you in there, you're going to act like you own the place because that's what you do. I don't know, maybe your mother didn't hug you enough or something, that's for you and your therapist to work out. What I'm saying is, if you walk in there with the assumption that you own the place, you'll start to think that you also own some of the *people* in there. Specifically the girls. Are you following me so far?"

Dickie crossed his arms. He didn't look happy, but he also didn't say anything. To do so would be to incriminate himself. At least he was smart enough to realize that.

"Now, I'm just a lowly security guard—heck, not even that, I'm a glorified bouncer—so I don't have the right to search you right now. But I'm willing to bet you have some…*vitamins* with you that make people *really* sleepy when you mix it with their drinks. Now I can't, in good conscience, let you in there to give someone a surprise catnap and God only knows what else. So, if you don't mind, I think it's best for you to carry on your merry way and go on home. Who knows? Maybe you'll be able to get to sleep without the help of those *vitamins.*"

"You think you're funny, slick? Spittin' lies 'bout me."

Tommy held up his finger. "Ah, let's review: I said they were *facts.*"

Dickie narrowed his eyes and stroked his chin as he slyly stepped back. "All right. I see how you work. You watch your back, boss. You're making enemies with the wrong people."

Tommy flashed him a smile. "I'll take my chances. Thanks

for stopping by. Drive safe getting home!"

Dickie glared at him, but turned away, offering cuss words to Tommy as he rounded the corner on the sidewalk and out of sight.

Tommy returned to his post by the door and stubbed out his cigarette with a smile. Kerry, his wife, will like this story. She always enjoyed Tommy's stories about how he outsmarted criminals or criminal-adjacent folks.

He wondered if she was asleep now or getting up for baby Laurel's late-night feeding. From what Tommy knew the few nights he got to spend at home, she usually woke up around two for a feeding. With Tommy working such strange hours in order to provide for them, Kerry always took the nightly feeding even though he was sure she was exhausted too.

But he helped out as much as he could when he was home. He wasn't one to sleep in, so he usually fed Laurel in the morning before he went off to work at the police station. Or, if he was home in the evenings, he gave her a bath so Kerry could have half an hour in front of the TV by herself.

Their situation wasn't ideal, but they were making the best of it. Kerry had been working for the city as a clerk, but with a shrinking population, she was let go. A few weeks after that she found out she was pregnant, which made finding another job harder. Especially one that would help pay for her maternity and childcare costs. Which meant that Tommy got a second job to make up for it.

Laurel would get older and Kerry would be able to go back to work eventually, but for the time being they had a rough road.

His thoughts were interrupted when he heard a shout from the alley beside the club. There was a side exit there in case of emergencies, but it was common knowledge that there was no alarm on the door, so some people used it to cut through the alley to the parking lot on West 5th Street.

With police instinct kicking in, Tommy rushed around the corner to see what the issue was. Moments later, as he was plunged into darkness, he briefly caught sight of Dickie's smug face before he felt the first punch.

CHAPTER 5

Kathy moved along with the beat as she danced in the dark club in a small area against the wall that she and Trisha claimed as their own. They each held their drinks up as they lost themselves in the music.

Throughout the night they had each garnered the notice of a few guys, but only one was granted Kathy's attention. He had black hair and dark features and when he smiled, dimples appeared on his cheeks that made her melt. But that could've been the alcohol slowly taking effect. She had had more than a few tequila sunrises, her go-to drink.

Kathy thought she heard him correctly when he leaned close to her ear and told her his name was Milo. She almost felt a little embarrassed to tell him her name, which wasn't nearly as exotic as his. He didn't seem to mind and offered his hand to dance, as if they were about to waltz. Compared to other couples on the dance floor grinding on each other, Kathy and Milo were fairly tame.

Just as Milo began to take braver steps and lean in to Kathy, Trisha nudged her arm.

Bathroom? she mouthed. It wasn't really a question.

Kathy turned back to Milo and smiled. She leaned in close to his ear. "I'll be right back. Don't lose our spot."

Trisha grabbed her hand and led her across the crowded room, weaving between erratic, drunken bodies to the line for the women's bathroom in the cramped hallway. Here they had at least a little reprieve from the head-splitting music.

"So you and Milo are getting along, huh?" Trisha asked as she dug through her purse and pulled out a compact mirror to examine her makeup.

"Oh, you know," Kathy replied coyly.

"Certainly getting over Jeremy," Trisha muttered as she fussed with her eye makeup and stepped forward in line. "This is the first night since we started going out that you've danced with a guy."

Kathy had been politely declining invitations from men for weeks. The very thought of it felt like she was betraying Jeremy, which was stupid because he was the one who broke up with her. But not because he didn't care about her, no matter what the Siren's magic revealed.

"Yeah, well, Milo's just—"

"Incredibly sexy," Trisha cut in. "Seriously, Kathy, if you don't take him home, I will."

Kathy laughed. "Not to be mean, but he's barely even looked in your direction all night."

"Oh, I could work my magic on him," she said. "But you have dibs. Make sure you take full advantage of that. Are you, you know, *prepared*?"

"For what?"

Trisha glanced over at her with her eyebrows raised.

"No!" Kathy exclaimed. "I'm not going home with anyone tonight and I'm not *taking* anyone home tonight."

"Whatever makes you feel good, girl." Trisha closed her compact and returned it to her purse. "Personally, if you're not looking to find a guy, I don't understand the point of going out."

"I mean, I like to dance."

"Everyone does. What you like is to window shop. You've got this guy in your cart! Get to the checkout."

Kathy laughed again, but her thoughts went to Jeremy. She didn't want to be the kind of girl who lingered on a guy who had broken up with her, but she couldn't help but hesitate and think about him whenever she was about to take a step with another guy.

Jeremy didn't break up with her because he didn't want to see her anymore. He just wanted space because she had been overbearing for a little while. She couldn't help but hold out hope that they would get back together.

She pinched the bridge of her nose and shook her head.

"Are you okay?" Trisha asked. "You're not going to puke, are you?"

"No, just trying to clear my head." *Get Jeremy out of it*, she thought. *I'm single. I have every right to dance with another guy and take it to whatever level I want.*

"You've had, like, four drinks. That didn't clear your head already?"

Kathy smiled and rolled her eyes.

"Hey, maybe Mr. Tall-Dark-and-Handsome will buy you one." Trisha winked.

After they made their way back to their spot, Kathy saw that Milo had two drinks in his hands. He raised one toward Kathy.

"Thought you could use one of these."

She took it. "You managed to save our spot *and* get me a drink?"

He smiled. "I have a few other tricks I could show you."

"Oh yeah? Like what?"

Leaning closer, she felt his hand on her back, pulling her in to his kiss. The rest of the room disappeared, the music faded to background noise, and Kathy lost herself in the moment. Gone were her thoughts about Jeremy and betraying the relationship that was over. Gone were her worries that she wasn't moving through life at the same speed as her sister. Gone was everything that had ailed her. For this moment, she was in pure bliss.

When he finally pulled away, her head was spinning and she could feel the effects of the four drinks. She staggered a little, but Milo's hand on her hip helped keep her in place.

"Are you okay?" he said at her ear. She could feel his breath against her skin and it took everything in her not to grab him and pull him in for another kiss.

Instead, she handed him the drink he offered her and leaned in to his ear. "I think I'm going to take off. Thanks for a fun night."

Milo pulled away, a sad expression on his face. "Are you sure?"

She nodded and looked around for Trisha, who had moved into the mob of dancers in the center of the room.

He held up his finger and gave her both drinks, then fished in his pockets for a pen. Snatching a cocktail napkin from a nearby table, he scrawled his phone number on it and wrote his name.

"Here," he said, taking the drinks back from her. "Give me a call and we can go somewhere and have a real conversation."

"I'd like that." She turned to leave, but he grabbed her arm and spun her around and kissed her again.

This time when she pulled away, she did feel a faint wave of nausea from the room spinning. She tried to stifle it, though, because the kiss was once again wonderful.

"I'll call you." Kathy waved the napkin at him and then turned to find her friend.

Bodies bounced into her as the effects of alcohol consumption removed personal boundary manners. Pushing her way through the crowd, Kathy reached out and nudged Trisha on the shoulder, who spun around quickly.

"What?"

Kathy nodded to the door and mouthed, *I'm going to go.*

Trisha held up a finger and pushed her way through the crowd to follow Kathy to the door.

"Here, let's just go through here," Trisha said. "It'll be easier than pushing our way to the front."

The side entrance was situated just before the hallway leading to the bathrooms. It was marked with a sign reading, "EMERGENCY EXIT, ALARM WILL SOUND," but everyone knew there was no alarm.

Trisha pushed through the door and out into the quiet night. Kathy felt immediate relief from no longer being in the stuffy club and somehow her head felt clearer, like fresh air had suddenly begun to sober her up, even though she knew that wasn't how it worked.

"Oh shoot!" Trisha said once they got outside.

"What?"

"I forgot to close my tab at the bar. They still have my credit card."

"Oh gotcha," Kathy said. "I'll wait out here."

"Are you sure?"

"I'll be fine, don't worry." She still knew how to use her

magic, no matter how inebriated she was. Not that Trisha knew that.

"I'll only be five minutes." She turned and as the door closed behind her, the music went from a loud celebration of life to a dull thumping sound.

Kathy crossed her arms across her chest and leaned against the wall. The door they exited out of was hidden behind a corner where the building extended further out into the alley, so the alley was wider near the back of the building than the front.

She tried to clear her head and take deep breaths to stem the nauseated feeling in her stomach. She hadn't lost her lunch yet on one of their outings and she wasn't about to start. Somehow Samantha would find out and it would be one more argument against Kathy going out and having fun. Even though she didn't voice it, Kathy knew her sister didn't approve of her outings.

With the ringing in her ears subsiding, Kathy became better atuned to the night sounds of the city around her. Most pressing of all was the sound of a scuffle from around the corner, closer to the street. One man grunting and breathing heavy. She listened closer. No, it was definitely two men.

Peering around the corner, she caught sight of a man hitting another man square in the face. The one who took the brunt of the punch fell to the ground, raising his arms in defense.

VALKYRIE

"Hey!" Kathy shouted at them. She took a step forward, but stopped when she noticed her bare leg and remembered what she was wearing. To creeps in an alley, her outfit shouted, *easy target.*

The man on the ground looked at her when she shouted, but the man standing seized the moment and delivered a final punch that flattened the other man, unmoving.

CHAPTER 6

The final blow took Kathy by surprise and she stood rooted to the ground where she was, not realizing at first that the man who gave the final punch had run off. She went from having fun and flirting with Milo to witnessing an attack in a matter of minutes.

Snapping out of it, she ran to the fallen man and crouched down next to him.

"Sir, can you hear me?" She watched his chest, watching for it to rise and fall. It did, but only slightly. His face was a bloody, swollen mess that made her stomach continue to turn. "Sir!"

She put her hand on his chest and could feel his breathing get weaker, irregular. "Sir, I'm going to go in and call for help. Hang in there. Keep breathing!"

Rising to her feet, she started to head back to the side entrance, but as she turned the corner, she caught a glimpse of someone else leaning over the man.

Stopping in her tracks, Kathy turned and saw it was a woman. It took another few seconds for it to sink in that she was dressed in warrior garb: bronze chest plate and a dark leather skirt with slits cut by the legs to prevent resistance when running. Her boots came up to her knee and she wore metals arm guards on her forearms. Her blonde hair flowed behind her in a mess of curls that made the size of her look larger than she was. Likely a sign that she packed a bigger punch than she seemed.

The oddly-dressed woman knelt beside the body and set the back of her hand on his unmoving chest. Raising it slowly in the air, Kathy watched as a translucent figure stepped up from the ground.

Once he was on his feet, Kathy recognized him: the bouncer from the entry of the club. Only, in his transparent form, he didn't have any of the abrasions that the body on the ground had.

The woman held out her hand and the man hesitated. She spoke something to him that Kathy couldn't make out. Finally, he grasped her hand and they turned toward the street.

"Where are you taking him?" Kathy called out.

The woman spun around, her eyes wide as she stared at the witch with surprise.

"I'm not going to let you take his spirit away," Kathy said. "He deserves to move on."

In response, the woman let go of the man's hand, set her feet firmly on the ground, and snarled at Kathy. The witch put up her hands to freeze the woman, but she was fast, dodging around the alley, leaping off the side of the neighboring building, and landing in front of Kathy.

The warrior woman didn't miss a beat and dropped to the ground to kick out Kathy's feet, sending her crashing to the ground as well. The woman jumped to her feet and pressed her boot against Kathy's chest.

"How can you see me?"

Kathy grabbed the woman's boot and tried twice to push it off, but the woman was strong and pushed harder against Kathy's chest after each attempt.

"What do you mean how can I see you?" Kathy asked through gritted teeth. "You're standing right there!"

The woman studied Kathy through narrow eyes. She held out her hand and a spear with a jagged rock tied to the end of it appeared in a puff of smoke. She swung it around and began to point the tip at Kathy's neck.

The side door burst open.

"Got it!" Trisha called out, then she saw Kathy. "What happened?" She rushed to help her friend up, seemingly oblivious of the warrior woman who was clearly not dressed for a night at the club.

The woman studied Trisha's reaction, then looked down at Kathy again and released her foot.

Kathy let Trisha help her up. "There was a guy here. Two guys, they got in a—"

"Is he dead?" Trisha shouted when she noticed the man laying on the ground.

Kathy followed her gaze and her heart sank. The woman returned to the translucent man and took his hand before they disappeared in a cloud of smoke.

She kicked herself for letting that woman take his spirit away. She knew for a fact he was dead and she felt guilty for not saving him. Would he have survived if she wasn't drunk and leaning against the building to keep her head from spinning instead of helping him fight off his attacker? Would she have been able to stop the fight before it started?

"Kathy, we have to call 9-1-1," Trisha said. "Are you sure you're okay?"

She nodded. "I'm okay."

Trisha grabbed her hand and led her back to the door. "I'm not leaving you alone again. Come on. We need to call someone."

CHAPTER 7

Surprisingly, Kathy had a clear head when she woke up the next morning. Maybe it was the four glasses of water she drank before bed or maybe it was the fact that she witnessed someone's murder and someone else take his soul. It really was a toss up.

After rushing across the hall to the bathroom to relieve herself of last night's hangover prevention, Kathy returned to her bedroom and crouched on the floor beside her bed. Their family magic book, *The Art of Magic*, rested just under her bed frame. It was a large leather-bound tome filled with crinkled pages on the magical encounters their family had had throughout the years. It was certainly their most treasured heirloom.

They really needed to find a better place for it other than under Kathy's bed.

She flipped open the cover, hearing the familiar creak of the spine. At the same time, her stomach grumbled loudly and she realized just how lightheaded she was. Maybe she did have a slight hangover after all.

Closing the book, she scooped it up in her arms and carried it downstairs. She could read and eat at the same time.

As she came down the stairs, she was surprised to hear the rustling of a newspaper coming from the kitchen. She stepped in and saw Samantha sitting at the kitchen table, coffee in hand, hunched over the morning paper. She was still in the powder blue T-shirt and white shorts she usually wore to bed. Her hair was starting to come loose from her bun.

"What are you still doing home?" Kathy set the book on the table beside her sister and crossed the room to pour herself a cup of coffee.

"Called in for this morning," Samantha said in an emotionless voice. "I told Mr. Marsden I'd be in around twelve."

"Why?" Kathy carried her mug over to the table and noticed her sister's red, puffy eyes. She had dark circles under them as well. "Honey, what's the matter?"

"Well, I told Steven I was a witch."

Kathy frowned. "And it didn't go well?"

Samantha motioned to herself. "Obviously not!"

Snippy, Kathy thought.

"Sorry," Samantha said. "It's just been a rough day."

It's eight a.m.

"I meant the last twenty-four hours!" Samantha said.

Kathy narrowed her eyes at her sister's response, but brushed it off. Instead, she leaned over behind Samantha's chair and wrapped her arms around her, squeezing her tight.

"I'm sorry he didn't react like you'd hoped. What did he say?"

"Well, he was mad that I didn't tell him."

Kathy slunk back over to her seat. "Can't blame him for that."

"I know, but it's not like I had a choice to keep it from him."

"You're preaching to the choir here."

"He needs space to process it all, which I can't argue with. I dumped a lot on him."

"How much of it were you able to explain before…" *Does he know that he might be a target in the future?* Kathy kept her real question to herself.

"I wasn't going to worry him about the dangers," Samantha said. "I want him to come around to the idea first."

"I'm sure he will."

"I'm not so sure." Samantha took a deep breath, desperate to change the subject. "Anyway, how was your night out? Did you have fun?"

"Yeah." Kathy got up from the table and went to the cupboard to pour herself a bowl of cereal.

Fun, if you don't count the man dying and the woman stealing his soul.

"Who died?"

"I didn't say anything about anyone dying," Kathy said.

Samantha pointed to her ears. "But I heard it!"

"Sam, I didn't *say* anything. What's going on with you? You were acting strange last night, too, before I left." She came back to the table and took a seat with her food.

Samantha sighed again. "Well, on top of everything going on with Steven, I think my powers are growing."

"That's good!" Kathy exclaimed, then saw her sister's annoyed look and changed her tone. "But apparently not. What am I missing?"

"I've been able to hear people's thoughts."

Kathy sat up straighter. "Even mine?"

"Uh-huh," Samantha said with a nod. "I have all this chatter up in my head and it's almost impossible to tell what someone's saying and what someone's thinking. It's why conversations with me have been so weird lately."

"Conversations with you are always weird." Kathy smirked.

Samantha swatted at her. "You know what I mean! This new power—or rather, this extension of my mind specialty—only made things worse when I talked to Steven yesterday."

"How so?"

"Well, there was a lot going through his head and I was picking up on it and responding to it," she explained. "Which made him think I was even more nuts than I am. I just wish it would go away. I'm already tired of hearing everyone's thoughts!"

Kathy grinned again. "Hearing voices that aren't there *is* a sign that someone's crazy."

"I'm serious here, Kathy!"

"I'm sorry, but you know the drill with new powers. They're like puppies. You have to get to know it and train it and work with it until you have a good grasp on its behavior. Think about when you first developed your persuasion ability. You thought you were the bee's knees and everyone was doing whatever you wanted until you realized what was going on. But you worked on it and focused it and now you have excellent control of when you dole out your persuasion."

"But I wasn't picking up on people's thoughts then! I mean, yesterday I found out that apparently Mr. Marsden is thinking of leaving his wife because I walked into his office when he was on the phone with a divorce lawyer. And the other day I was at the grocery store and I overheard the cashier counting down how many hours he had left in his shift. Hell, even at a red light yesterday I heard the thoughts of someone in the car next to me. It's endless!"

"Because this is new," Kathy pushed. "Samantha, you'll get the hang of it. Cut yourself some slack. You know for a fact this will work to our advantage with the bad guys we face." *I wonder if she can see things play out in people's minds or just hear conscious thoughts?*

"Right now, just conscious thoughts."

Kathy made a face. "Creepy. Stop doing that with me. I don't like you hearing what's going on in my head. It's an invasion of privacy."

"Trust me, I want to get a handle on this as soon as I can. The sooner I can control when my telepathy kicks in and when it doesn't, the happier I'll be."

"So do you think in the future you might be able to *see* people's thoughts?"

"Maybe," Samantha speculated. "I don't know. This new extension confirms that my specialty is the mind. Who knows where that will take me."

"Weird."

"Yeah. Now, what happened last night? Obviously something supernatural if you brought down the book."

Kathy finished her breakfast and pushed the dishes aside to bring the book closer to her. "Well, the night was going great. We met this guy, Milo, and he was sweet and cute and he bought me a few drinks."

Samantha leaned on her fist and raised her eyebrows.

"Nothing happened further than that." Kathy bit her lip. "Well, we kissed and it was—it was good. Really good." *I wish I would've invited him back and—*

Samantha snapped her fingers at her sister. "Kathy! Remember I can hear what you're thinking!"

"Gross."

"For you and me both." She tapped a page in *The Art of Magic*. "Let's get back to why you pulled this out."

"Anyway, Trisha and I decided to call it a night and we went through the side exit into the alley."

Samantha cringed. "How drunk were you?"

"Well, I did say that Milo was buying me drinks."

"Do you know how dangerous that could've been?"

"All right, *Mom*. Just listen. Trisha went back in to get her card—"

"And left you outside?"

"Drunk or not, I still knew how to use my powers!"

Samantha gave her sister another disapproving look, but let her continue.

"Anyway," Kathy went on as she flipped through the pages of the magic book, "I heard these two guys fighting and I called out to them, which is when the one guy hauled off and hit the other one."

"Was he okay?"

"Well…I don't—I don't know."

"What do you mean?"

"The one guy ran off," Kathy explained. "So I rushed to the guy on the ground and he didn't look good. He had been beat up pretty bad. I turned to go back into the club to call for help, but then I saw this woman appear."

"Woman? What woman? Like witch?"

"I don't think so. Like…" Kathy stopped on a page marked *Valkyries*. "Like them!"

Samantha turned so she could read the passage. There was a drawing of a group of women dressed in armor and leather. They each had fierce looks and their hair blew behind them.

With roots in Norse mythology, valkyries are immortal women who collect the souls of fallen heroes to bring to Valhalla, the Hall of the Slain. There, the fallen heroes prepare for Ragnarök, the final battle between the gods and their enemies that would result in the old world being destroyed to make way for a new one.

Typically, valkyries are invisible to everyone in Midgard (our world), however, it is believed that by changing your state of mind, the cloak of magic maintaining the valkyries' secrecy could be unveiled.

"Are you sure this is who you saw?" Samantha asked. "It says here they should be invisible."

"I'm positive. She must've been collecting that man's soul." *And attacked me because she was surprised I saw her.*

"She attacked you?"

"Only until Trisha came out and saw me on the ground."

"And *she* didn't see the woman?"

"Not that I could tell."

"But *you* saw her?"

Kathy nodded. "That would be why I'm looking in the book."

Point taken. "How?"

"Well, if this passage is to be believed, it's probably because I'm a witch, coupled with the fact that last night I wasn't in my right mind."

"You're saying you saw her because you were *drunk*?"

Kathy shrugged. "What are the odds that a drunk witch would see a heroic man die and a valkyrie collect his soul? Those are very specific circumstances that don't usually correlate. It was just a freak accident."

"But then why would she attack you?"

"Because I called out to her. Maybe she was afraid that her invisibility had been removed for some reason. She ran off when Trisha came out because she realized it was still intact."

"Maybe." Samantha tried not to worry about it, but worrying was in her nature.

"By the sounds of it, the valkyrie I saw last night was just doing her job. That man was dead. I wish I could've saved him, but I spotted the fight too late. At least now his soul will serve a higher purpose."

"Based on what's in the book, I hope that higher purpose doesn't happen for a long time."

Kathy closed the book. "Well, that answers that. Valkyries are no more a threat to people than witches are."

"Good. Let me get a handle on this new power before any

other supernatural foes try to kill us."

Kathy folded her arms on the book and laid her head down. "I just wish things could've been different."

"If that man was meant to die, there's nothing you could've done differently," Samantha said. "You tried to help him. Besides, as you said, you weren't in the right state of mind to be helping anyone."

Kathy picked up her head and shot her sister a look. "If I *was* in my right state of mind, I would've been able to chase after his attacker. Maybe make it easier for the police to get him and arrest him."

Samantha shook her head. "That's not our job as witches. We need to protect people from ill-intentioned *magical* people. Not thugs on the street downtown. Save that for the police."

"I know. I just wish it was different."

"Look, the police are not going to take this lightly," Samantha said. "Trust me, they'll find the guy who did this. But that's *their* job, not ours."

Kathy sighed. "Yeah, I know."

Samantha carried her mug to the sink. "I'm going to take a shower. What are you up to today?"

"Nothing much. I have to work tomorrow so I'm counting today as my Saturday."

"Well, I'll be out of your hair shortly." Samantha came over and hugged her sister from behind. "Thanks for talking me off the ledge about Steven."

"Anytime."

After Samantha left, Kathy opened *The Art of Magic* again and turned back to the page on the valkyries. She studied the image, replaying the events of last night in her head.

You better not be an enemy, Kathy thought. *Samantha is too fragile right now to handle another threat.*

CHAPTER 8

Kathy finished off her run with a walk down the next two blocks to cool her down. The summer heat was relentless and she was soaked in sweat. The only thing that kept her going was the thought of drinking an ice cold glass of water and taking a nice cool shower when she got home.

She thought her run would help distract her from the events of last night, but her mind seemed laser-focused on it. She couldn't keep the man who died out of her head. Even though Samantha had reminded Kathy that there was nothing else she could do, she knew what happened last night would have ripple effects on everyone who knew him. His family, friends, the people he worked with. Surely, that man had people who cared about him and relied on him and would miss him now that he was gone. She wished there was something she could do to bring them comfort, but she knew there was nothing.

Hopefully the people he left behind would remember him as someone who was noble. The valkyries wouldn't have taken him if he wasn't.

The valkyries intrigued her. Their invisibility, the fact that she saw one of them, and the battle of Ragnarök. All of it was a mystery to her. What other worlds and ways of life were out there that she had no idea about? Ones that were right under her nose.

Not that she could talk. She and Samantha were witches living amongst people who didn't believe in them. Some of their neighbors *couldn't* believe in them. Was Steven one of them?

As Kathy climbed the steps to her house and fished the spare key out of the bottom of the mailbox, she worried about the future of Samantha's relationship. Maybe Kathy had been putting Steven and Samantha's love on a higher pedestal than it deserved. If Steven couldn't accept the fact that Samantha was a witch, did he really accept her completely? That didn't seem like the foundation of a good marriage to Kathy, not that she had experience or examples of good marriages.

She let herself into the house, poured herself the reward of an ice cold glass of water, and stood in front of a fan for five minutes as she drank it.

After taking a shower and changing into something comfortable to go about her day in the heat, she decided to be productive on her day off and go to the library to read up on the valkyries. They might not be a threat, but now that she knew they were real, she wanted to know the mythology behind them. Maybe add to the entry in the magic book for future generations who come in contact with them.

Kathy stepped out the front door and started down Arlington Road to the Cherry Street bus stop. If she hurried, she would still be able to make 1:23 bus.

As she walked, she could already feel the sweat dripping down her back and she dreaded getting on the bus filled with other sweaty people. But the library would have air conditioning, so it was only for a short while.

Kathy approached the intersection with Homeland Boulevard, only one block away from the bus stop. It was shaded by mature trees and bushes growing up in the yards of neighboring houses. At first, Kathy relished in the relief from the sun's rays, until the scent of smoke turned her attention behind her.

The valkyrie from the night before stood only a few feet away, dressed in her full warrior attire.

Kathy froze her, but two more valkyries appeared in a puff of smoke, boxing Kathy in. She put up her hands and froze them as well, but was horrified when she saw them push against her magic slowly, then break through it altogether as if she hadn't used her power on them at all.

"We are servants of the god Odin," the one from the night

before said. "Your magic won't last with us."

"Okay, okay—look." Kathy put up her hands in surrender. "I know you're not bad. I know you were only doing your job last night. I just—"

Another valkyrie stepped up and reached for her arm, but Kathy swatted her away.

"Hey!" Kathy shouted out. This was one of the rare moments she hoped one of the neighbors would hear and come out to look, scaring the valkyries off. But there was no such luck today. "Look, I know you were supposed to be invisible, but trust me, last night was just a fluke. A coincidence. A way for me to appreciate the importance of your duty as valkyries." She was rambling, fishing for anything that would keep them at bay and keep their hands off of her.

The valkyries exchanged glances with one another while they kept Kathy boxed in.

"She knows who we are," one of them said.

"It must be a sign," another said.

"Ladies," the one from last night announced. "She fought back yesterday, so some force will be required."

Sensing what was coming, Kathy tried her magic again, but it had no effect at all on the valkyries this time. She ducked as they each swung at her and slipped between two of them. If she could get to Cherry Street where there was more traffic and more eyes, maybe the valkyries would go away on their own and she could stay in a crowd until she could get to Samantha to—

VALKYRIE

One of the valkyries grabbed her shoulder and yanked her back as she tried to run. She stumbled, but remained on her feet, even as another one delivered a kick to her side.

Kathy swung around and delivered her own kick back to the valkyrie, but another grabbed her from behind and restrained her arms. The witch struggled, eventually breaking free of the valkyrie's hold, but she stumbled to the ground in the process.

The third valkyrie, the one from last night, towered over Kathy and put a foot on her chest, just as she did only twelve hours earlier. She pushed Kathy on her back in the middle of the street.

Within seconds, Kathy saw the other two valkyries tower over her with their hands on their hips and she knew she didn't stand a chance. These women were warriors. *Trained* warriors. Kathy only knew basic self-defense.

"Get up, witch," the one from the night before said. "And do not try anything. It is time you give us some answers."

One of the valkyries standing over her forced Kathy to her feet, keeping her arms restrained behind her. The witch gave half a mind to kicking the one standing directly in front of her, but she knew how that would pan out.

The other two valkyries approached, resting their hands on each other's shoulders. Together, the four of them disappeared in a puff of smoke.

CHAPTER 9

Tommy woke up in a well-lit, well-furnished room. The walls were made up of white panels inset with gold trim. Along them, he saw photographs, which, upon closer inspection, he realized were of his family. His wife, daughter, parents. Close friends and neighbors. Co-workers from the station. Nearly everyone he cared about was photographed in one way or another—in photos Tommy didn't even remember having taken. Yet another thing to add to the list of mysteries.

The bed he woke up on was framed by a golden headboard, intricately detailed in the shape of two trees with their branches melding together. The sheets were red and silky smooth. The mattress was plush, made for complete relaxation.

On the other side of the room, there was a table filled with fruit, bread, cheese, and two decanters: one with water and one with what looked to be wine. All of the offerings were laid out in an elegant way, as if presented for a dinner party. But Tommy was alone, he knew that much.

Most importantly, he noticed two doors. One opened to a large bathroom with tiled floors, gold trimmings, and a marble bathtub. On a hook hung his police uniform, which was curious to him.

The other door wouldn't budge. He was sure that was the way out, too. He yanked on the golden doorknob—also intricately designed, this time as a horse's head—but it didn't move.

Frustrated, he looked up at the sunlight streaming through the windows at the top of the wall near the high ceiling. There were thick roman columns barricading him in and he looked to the display of food, wondering if he could use one of the plates to chip away the columns and free himself.

Of course, that was if he could even reach the windows. Tommy looked around the room for something to stand on or stack, but everything looked heavy or otherwise unmovable. And it was. He started with the table, which, after summoning all of his strength and getting the right footing, only moved an inch. The bed surely wouldn't be any help, either.

Just as he was considering pulling up the mattress and looking at how the bed was assembled, the second door opened and a woman dressed in metal and leather stepped in.

"I see you are awake," she said.

She seemed to have no shame about the fact that the slits in her skirt, which parted for her muscular legs, were cut very high. Her biceps were well-defined too. Tommy thought they were probably even bigger than his, not that he would admit that out loud. The woman's blonde hair was braided and hung down her back, stopping just before the waist of her skirt.

"Who are you?" he asked. "And where the hell am I?"

"My name is Eir," she said. "I guess you could say I am a sort of welcoming committee for new warriors to Valhalla."

He narrowed his eyes. "Valhalla?"

"Yes, the Hall of the Slain."

His face displayed utter confusion.

Eir motioned to the bed. "Sit. Let me explain."

Cautiously, Tommy took a seat on the red sheets. *Hall of the Slain?* he asked himself. *Does that mean I'm dead? Maybe that's why there are pictures of my family on the walls.*

"Are you hungry?" She waved to the table of food. "All of this is yours to eat. It will not ever spoil, so no need to worry about that. If it is not to your liking, I could—"

"I need answers."

Eir crossed her arms and pursed her lips, looking down to the floor.

"I'm sorry," he said. "I'm just—I have no idea what's going on."

"None of the warriors ever do," she said.

"Warriors? Why do you keep calling me that?"

"Because that is what you are. You were a hero on Midgard, which has made you a valuable asset to us. Unfortunately for you, your time in Midgard has come to an end, but now you can serve a higher purpose in your afterlife before moving on."

Tommy rubbed his face in his hands. This had to be a dream. None of it made any sense. But it all looked so *real*. And what was the last thing he remembered before waking up in here? He couldn't recall.

"Midgard?" he asked. "What's that."

"The human world," she replied. "I suppose you would call it Earth."

"So I'm not on Earth anymore?"

"No."

"Then where am I?"

"I told you, Valhalla."

"Right, but *where* is Valhalla?"

She smiled. "Oh, my mistake. I misunderstood you. Valhalla is in Asgard, home of the gods. Some of them, at least."

"The gods…" he murmured, skeptical. *What did I eat before I went to bed? And* when *did I go to bed?* "So why am I here? I'm not a god."

Eir chuckled. "No, you most certainly are not. You are a spirit who will help fight in the final battle of Ragnarök against Loki and the giants."

High school mythology started to come back to him.

"Ragnarök? So that would make you—"

"A valkyrie." She nodded. "We are servants of Odin, who is the god of war. Our job is to find fearless heroes, such as yourself, and collect their souls upon their death. We bring their souls here, to Valhalla, and train them to be warriors for Ragnarök, or the Twilight of the Gods."

"So you want to train me?"

She nodded.

"Then where's the battlefield? Why am I given such a plush room?"

"You will be shown to the arena very soon," she said. "We like to give our new warriors a little bit of special treatment, such as this room. You will join the other warriors in their barracks tomorrow. This room is to help you adjust to your newfound legacy."

"But you said I was a hero," he said. "I didn't do anything heroic—"

"I would have to disagree," Eir said. "While Asgard is drastically different from Midgard, our job as valkyries is to pay attention to the way you live your life in your world. We know you were a police officer, a protector. We have even brought your uniform here for you to wear as you train and when you fight the final battle."

Well, that explained that. "But I've only been a cop for a few years," he said. "It wasn't that long ago that I was still in the academy."

"Regardless of your time served, you acted with virtue, with heart, and with passion. All of which we look for in our own warriors. Even if your time with the police was short, you made a difference. You saved lives. You stopped ill-intentioned people. And you maintained peace. All qualities of a hero, in my book."

Tommy was quiet. He didn't know what to say. He hadn't thought of it in the way she just explained. He was only doing his job. Waking up, going to work each morning, just like everyone else. He didn't do it for praise or notoriety.

"We have warriors here who have spent their time on Midgard as soldiers, leaders, protectors. We have warriors from all walks of life, all colors, all cultures, and all time periods. We have been preparing for this for a long time and we believe you are the perfect fit for our mission before you are granted eternal peace."

He studied her, taking in her words, unsure of what else to say. It was all so much to take in. No wonder they had a room designated for people to process this. And, he had to admit, having the photos of his friends and family helped—especially the ones of his wife and daughter.

"We did not decide that it was the end of your time in Midgard," Eir went on. "But we were there when it was. To give you a chance to fulfill a greater destiny than your time in your world allowed."

His eyes widened. "Wait a minute. I'm…dead, aren't I?"

"In the physical sense, yes. You will never be able to return to Midgard and interact with anyone there as you have once done."

Tommy felt a lump forming in his throat as he thought of who he left behind. His wife, now a single mother without a job. His daughter, who was only a baby and would grow up without knowing who her father was. He thought of all the experiences that he would miss out on. Things that he was looking forward to. His daughter's first words, the first time she walked, her first day of school, all of it. Anniversaries with his wife. More children. Trips with his family.

It was all gone. Taken from him.

He buried his head in his hands as the pain of it erupted out of him. It was a weird feeling, mourning his own death. But here he was—something that even his wildest dreams couldn't have even thought up—and this was his new reality.

"I will give you some time to process all of this," Eir said. "I will be back later." She opened the door and left.

Tommy remained where he was, hunched over on the side of the bed, crying for the loss of his family, his friends, and his life.

CHAPTER 10

The valkyries marched Kathy through a brick hallway that had appeared in after she was taken from the street back in Erie. She tried to free herself, but it was no use. There were simply more valkyries and they were definitely stronger than she was.

Down the hall, she could hear the roar of what sounded like a crowd. As they approached the opening, the clatter of metal hitting metal and the firing of ammunition added to the collective noise.

What the hell is going on? she thought to herself.

The valkyries led her to an opening, where she stepped onto a sandy floor in a wide open arena where the source of the noise was. She stared up at the tall brick walls surrounding her. Took in the crowd, sectioned off and fighting with one another, slowly gaining interest in the newcomer entering the arena. As they took notice, the collective noise seemed to subside until most of the warriors in the arena stood staring as the valkyries dragged Kathy in.

She tried to look around, to plan her escape, or seek out any allies, but within a minute of entering the arena, she was tossed into a cage along the brick wall off the hallway. The heavy metal door slammed closed behind her.

Quickly, she hurried to the door trapping her inside. She wrapped her hands around the thick metal bars.

"Hey! You can't just leave me here!" she demanded. "What the hell is going on?"

Another valkyrie appeared to her right from out of view and handed a large bowl to one of the valkyries who had captured Kathy. She slid the bowl through an opening in the bars. After it passed through, the opening sealed shut with a bright light, killing any hope Kathy had of getting out of there.

Kathy peered inside the bowl. There was a loaf of bread and a hunk of cheese. "What's this?"

The valkyries ignored her and turned back to the crowd in the arena.

"Hey!" Kathy shouted out again. "Tell me what the hell is going on!" Her eyes flickered around the arena, but her mind was racing with all kinds of other thoughts and worries.

Still, the word *Valhalla* came to her amongst everything else going through her mind. Valkyries were connected with Valhalla, which was probably where she was. At least that was one thing figured out.

"I'm going to get out of here," she went on. "You're going to wish you hadn't—"

One of the valkyries turned, swung open the cage door, and slammed her forearm down hard on Kathy's neck. Her vision went black and she collapsed onto the sandy floor.

CHAPTER 11

It was rare that Samantha got a quiet night alone at home. Especially since her mind specialty had expanded, she hadn't had a moment to decompress with just her thoughts. And there were a lot of them. So tonight, she relished in the fact that she no longer had chatter in her head.

After fixing herself a quick TV dinner, she plopped on the couch with a book she'd been meaning to read and enjoyed the peace and quiet. As much as she tried to put him out of her mind, she couldn't help but worry about her future with Steven. They hadn't spoken since he stormed out last night.

Would she have more quiet nights like these? Alone in the house with no one to keep her company except a good book. Would she get a cat for company?

It would be fitting, she thought. *A witch who has a cat.*

Perhaps she'd even take up knitting and completely turn into a crazy cat lady spinster. One who fought evil and saved the world on occasion.

Setting her book down, she looked out the window into the dark night. Maybe magic could help her and Steven. Whether that be by seeing what their future held or convincing him that her being a witch wasn't that big of a deal.

Does such a spell even exist? she thought.

Samantha shook her head. She wasn't an enchantress, so she wouldn't be able to use magic to manipulate the subtle nuisances of love. And even if she could, she didn't want to go into a marriage knowing that her husband had been under a spell in order to take those vows.

Returning to her book, she finished the chapter she was reading and then stuck her bookmark in between the pages and set it down. She had managed to read half of the book. Since she no longer had plans for her Saturday, she figured she could read the rest tomorrow.

Getting up from the couch, she went into the kitchen for a glass of water and noticed the time. Almost midnight. She'd been reading longer than she thought. Kathy still wasn't home.

Earlier, Kathy had told Samantha that she wasn't up to much today because she had to work tomorrow.

So why isn't she home? Samantha wondered. *Did Trisha call her at the last minute to go out? Wouldn't be the first time that's happened. Kathy's been a social butterfly since she and Jeremy broke up.*

Reaching for the phone, she started to dial Trisha's number, but put the phone back in the cradle before she finished. Kathy would've left a note if she was going out with Trisha. And if they were going to a bar or a club—which was typically what Kathy did when she got together with Trisha—they wouldn't have left until after Samantha got home.

Unless Kathy doesn't want me to know where she is.

Picking up the phone again, she called Jeremy's apartment. It rang and rang and rang until a groggy voice answered.

"Hello?" a man's voice said, but not Jeremy's.

"Hi, this is Samantha, Kathy's sister," she started. "Sorry to be calling so late, but she wouldn't happen to be over there with Jeremy, is she?"

"No, she's not here," he said. "Neither is he. Do you want me to have him call you when he gets in?"

Samantha considered it, just so she could know where Kathy was, but she reminded herself that she was her sister, not her mother. Kathy had every right to do what she wanted and be with whomever she wanted. "No, that's okay. Sorry again. I'll catch up with her later. Thanks."

"Yeah."

Setting the phone back down, Samantha wondered where else Kathy could be. But then, it would make sense that if she went back to Jeremy she'd want to keep it quiet. And Samantha didn't want to make her feel bad about that decision, even if she did think it was a bad one.

Shrugging it off, Samantha turned off the lights and went up to bed. Kathy was working the next day, so Samantha would know where she was then. And she'd need a ride home too.

I need to stop worrying, she thought to herself. *I'll pick Kathy up from work tomorrow and she'll tell me where she's been.*

At least, that was the hope. Samantha might not be her mother, but she knew she would sleep better if she knew that Kathy was somewhere safe and sound for the night.

CHAPTER 12

Tommy had finally calmed down after coming to the realization that he was dead. He laid back on the ornate bed and stared up at the ceiling, painted with figures fighting in the clouds. He had put on his police uniform, for no other reason than it was familiar. And it was here, which had to mean something.

Is this the final battle Eir was talking about? he wondered. *Is that what she wants me to be a part of?*

He didn't know how that'd be possible. But then, he didn't understand anything now that he was dead. All of this was new to him.

There was a soft knock on the door and then Eir entered. Tommy quickly sat up, dropping his feet back onto the floor.

"How are you feeling?" she asked.

He shrugged. "Okay, I guess."

She nodded. "It will come and go in waves, much like grief. What will help is keeping yourself busy. Are you ready to learn about your new destiny?"

Tommy narrowed his eyes. "I just have a few more questions."

"Of course." She stood at attention with her hands behind her back and her chest puffed out.

"What exactly *is* Ragnarök? I mean, I know it's the final battle, but…" He looked up. "Is that it?"

"That is one interpretation, yes," she said. "The truth is, we do not know for sure. There are rumors, prophecies, and predictions, but until it happens, we cannot be sure."

"So how do you know you need an army?"

Eir bowed her head for a moment and then met his eyes. "Consider this: you did not know what the afterlife would be like. You theorized what it would be: pearly gates, eternal paradise. But until you got here, you could not be sure. It is the same with Ragnarök."

"So this is heaven?"

She smiled. "No, this is Valhalla."

"I know that. It's just—" He groaned and plopped back on the side of the bed, burying his head into his hands. "I don't understand how someone like me could fight for the gods. Or why you even want me to."

"Oh," she said with another subtle nod. "I see. Well, as I explained before, Ragnarök is the final battle between the gods of Asgard, where Valhalla is located, and the enemies of the gods, specifically Loki and the giants."

"Again, not seeing how I could help."

"It is in several prophecies that Loki will not only be recruiting giants to help him raid Asgard, but other beings and creatures as well. And lets not forget, there are strength in numbers. Myself and the other valkyries have been preparing for this battle for centuries. We have acquired a very skilled army."

"And what happens if we fail?"

"At least you will have failed knowing that you put forth your best effort," Eir said. "That is all we can ask for. I do not think you have anything to worry about. We will provide you with proper training, but we need to act quickly."

"Why? You said I could take my time."

"Circumstances have changed," she said. "Ragnarök may be happening sooner than we thought, in a way that is different than we thought. You will not have as much time to train as the other warriors, but I promise, you will be prepared." She extended her hand. "Let me take you on a tour of Valhalla to help get you acquainted before we put you in training. We do not have much time."

Tommy looked at her hand and then up into her eyes. "What if I refuse?"

"You will not refuse. Sooner or later, you will come to terms with your destiny. However, I warn you: the longer it takes for you to decide to join us, the less time you will have to feel prepared. We have trained confident, brave warriors and we believe you have the qualities that align with the rest of our army. But there are certain preparations that need to be made first."

Again, he hesitated. Eir hadn't given him specifics, but even if she had, would it be something he understood? They were so far removed from his idea of normal—a whole new world, in fact—that nothing that happened to him would surprise him. But how could he just take her for her word?

"What do I get out of this?" he asked.

"Not only will you have the satisfaction of knowing you lived a full life, even in the afterlife, but once Ragnarök is over, you will be able to move on to a place where you will be able to watch over your wife and daughter."

"I can't do that here in Asgard?"

"Not as easily as you could once you move on, no."

"But what if this final battle doesn't come for several more centuries?" he asked. "I'll still miss out on my family's life."

"It will not be several centuries before this battle takes place," Eir said. "Something has happened that we believe is a sign that Ragnarök is upon us. Your timing is impeccable, Mr. Wilson. You will not have to wait long for the afterlife." She extended her hand again. "Are you ready to begin your next journey?"

Tommy studied her a moment longer, but grasped her hand

and stood. He might not know where he was going to end up, but he couldn't spend forever in this room. If there was even a slim chance that he'd see his family again, he needed to take it.

CHAPTER 13

Kathy's head was still pounding when the sunlight finally crested over the top of the arena wall. It had been a rough night sleeping on the sandy floor, trapped in what appeared to be a five-by-five foot cage. She woke up in the middle of the night to pitch-darkness and total silence. There were no signs of the valkyries anywhere—or *anyone* for that matter—and the only thing left for her to do at that point was to try to get some sleep and save her energy for when she did see them again.

Through the night, she tried to get comfortable by curling up in the fetal position or laying diagonally in her cage, but it wasn't the most ideal circumstances for sleep. Not to mention the overwhelming worry she had about where she was, what the valkyries wanted, and whether or not she would ever get out. It all disrupted what little sleep she had been able to get.

Reaching for the meal that had been provided for her when she arrived, Kathy picked at the stale bread and really took in her surroundings for the first time since her arrival.

Her cage was in a large arena with an open roof and a sandy floor. There were chambers tucked in along the wall, of which her cage was in one of them. If she had to guess, she would've thought she was in the Roman Colosseum before it fell into ruins. Except, this arena didn't have observation seating for matches. That, Kathy was grateful for. She hoped it meant that the valkyries weren't going to make her fight for her freedom.

In one of the chambers on the other side of the arena, Kathy could make out what appeared to be the armory. Beside that was a marble fountain with metal ladles hooked on the edge for drinking. She was suddenly very aware of how dry her mouth was. The bread and cheese breakfast wasn't helping.

If I could get over there and get a good drink of water I'd have more energy and a clearer head to think, she thought to herself. *And if I could get into that armory...*

What she still couldn't wrap her head around was why the valkyries hunted her down and brought her to Valhalla at all. From what she read in the book, valkyries didn't interact with people in her world. Did this have anything to do with the fact that she saw one of them the other night at the club?

From one end of the arena, a door clanged open and the

sound of chatter carried in as a large crowd of men walked in and headed straight for the armory. They were an odd bunch. People of all different colors, backgrounds, and time periods, dressed in clothes that represented their culture instead of a unified valkyrie army. Everything from camouflage and helmets to armor and chain mail.

When they emerged from the armory equipped with weapons, Kathy could see there were men wearing bright formal coats brandishing rifles with bayonets and women in plainclothes wielding handguns, among other configurations. They all seemed out of place at first glance, but as they moved into groups, working with each other wielding similar weapons and other forms of warfare, Kathy could see a seamless sense of congruency between them.

At least our book got one thing right, she thought. *There is an army being trained.*

Among that army, Kathy spotted one of the valkyries who attacked her on Homeland Boulevard back in Erie.

"Hey!" Kathy pressed herself against the bars of her cage and waved the valkyrie over. "I want to talk to you!"

The valkyrie had a stern look on her face and when she turned, Kathy could see she was holding a long spear in her hand. She marched over to the cage.

"What do you want?" she snarled.

"I want you to let me out of here!" Kathy banged on the bars. "I have no reason to be in here!"

"Wrong! This is exactly where you deserve to be!" the valkyrie retorted.

"Why? What did I do?" she asked.

"It is not what you did, it is what you saw. How were you able to see Herja collect Thomas Wilson's soul?"

"Herja?" Kathy asked. "Is that the name of the valkyrie?" She didn't realize they had names, but it made sense. Everyone had a name.

"Yes, now how did you see her?"

"What's your name?" Kathy pushed. "I'm Kathy. I'm a witch." She extended her hand, but the valkyrie slapped it hard with the side of her spear, causing the witch to quickly retract her hand back to herself.

"Brynhildr," she responded. "Now do not reach through those bars again unless you want to lose an arm."

Kathy nodded.

"How were you able to see Herja?"

"It was an accident," she started. "This is all just a misunderstanding. See, I went out that night and I had a few drinks and I think maybe it's possible that that combined with
" Something in the crowd of practicing warriors caught her eye. The man she watched die not even two days ago was walking around the arena with another valkyrie. "Is that the man from before? The one who died? If he's dead, then how is he…? Am *I* dead?"

Brynhildr slapped the bars on her cage with her spear and a

loud clang erupted. "No, you are not dead, witch. Only the members of our army have died. We have never allowed true mortals in here until now."

"I'm a witch!"

"But you will die like a human, will you not?"

Kathy gulped. "Um…I suppose so. Look, if you'll just hear me out, I think we can clear all of this up and you can just let me go on home—"

"You are not going home," Brynhildr said. "And you are going to listen to *me*. How were you able to see Herja?" Her voice grew into a growl.

"Well, I said I had had a lot to drink that night—"

"We all drink," Brynhildr cut in. "It makes no difference."

She must not understand what I meant by drinking, Kathy thought. *Maybe if I told her that it's alcohol—*

"Are you working for Loki?"

"Loki?" Kathy echoed. "I don't even know who that is! No, I'm not!"

"I do not see any other explanation for this," she countered. "None of the valkyries have ever been spotted before. Why are you so special? Unless you are working for Loki and the giants."

"No, you've got it all wrong. It was a very unique circumstance that must not have ever happened before. If you'll just let me explain—"

"There is no time to explain," Brynhildr cut in again. "Thanks to you, we have a lot of work to do." She turned to leave, but Kathy called out to her again.

"Wait! What do you mean thanks to me you have work to do? What did I even do?"

Brynhildr spun around but didn't come any closer. "As I have said, a valkyrie has never been seen before while collecting a soul. That must mean that Ragnarök has begun much earlier than we anticipated. We need to get our warriors ready for the final battle."

"No! This isn't what it looks like!" Kathy called out to her, but the valkyrie kept walking through the crowd of fighting warriors. "Come back!"

It was too late. Brynhildr had moved on out of earshot. Kathy sat back in her cage and hoped that her desire to have a night out with Trisha didn't just start the end of the world.

CHAPTER 14

When Samantha opened her bedroom door in the morning, the first thing she noticed was that Kathy's was still wide open. Peeking her head in her sister's room, she saw the bed was still made as if it hadn't been slept in at all. More surprising was that Samantha didn't hear the thought chatter from anyone else in the house. Kathy wasn't home.

Then she remembered that Kathy was supposed to be working and if she didn't come home last night, she probably got a ride into work with whoever she ended up with the night before.

Padding into the bathroom, Samantha turned on the water in the shower. Hopefully it would help clear her mind and put her at ease. She didn't feel any less stress than she did the night before. Not that she was expecting any relief, being that none of her problems had been miraculously fixed while she slept. Steven was still turned off by the idea that she was a witch. Kathy still hadn't gotten in touch with her. And as far as Samantha knew, she could still read people's minds.

After her shower, Samantha dressed and went downstairs for breakfast. Her hair was still damp. It was too hot to blow-dry it.

When she stepped into the kitchen, she noticed the magic book was still sitting on the table. She had overlooked it the night before when she went to bed, but here it was screaming at her, as if it were a sign that needed to be noticed.

Kathy had been M.I.A. since Samantha left for work yesterday. What if something happened to her?

You're being paranoid, Samantha thought.

Ignoring the intuition that told her that something was wrong, Samantha fixed herself a cup of coffee and popped some bread into the toaster. As she stirred in the sugar and creamer, she glanced over at the book, her mind running wild again.

What if Kathy was in trouble? What if the valkyries weren't as harmless as they thought? What if someone she met at the club somehow figured out where she lived and did something to her? What if that someone she met at a club convinced her to come to his house and then drugged her? What if Kathy went to help Trisha and ended up getting hurt herself?

Why didn't Samantha call Trisha last night?

Before she knew what she was doing, she had the phone in her hand and was dialing in Trisha's number.

It rang twice before she picked up, sounding groggy. "Hello?"

"Trisha? It's Samantha Walker, Kathy's sister. Did I wake you?"

"Hi Sam." She yawned. "You did, but that's okay. I need to be in work in, like, an hour and I didn't set my alarm."

"Were you out last night? With Kathy?"

"I did go out last night, but I didn't see Kathy," Trisha said. "Why?"

"Nothing, I just haven't heard from her, that's all. Did she meet anyone when you guys went out on Thursday? Or did she talk about going to see anyone last night?"

"No, she didn't say anything," Trisha said. "She did meet a guy on Thursday, but as far as I know she only took his number."

Would Kathy call him up and meet him on her own? Perhaps she would consider it in the middle of the day. But people who are bad at night can be equally sinister during the day too. He might've done something to her or given her something that—

"Do you think something happened to her?" Trisha asked.

"I'm probably just overreacting," Samantha said. "Just thought I'd check. You wouldn't happen to have that guy's number, would you?"

"No. But I want to say his name was Matteo or Milo or something."

"Okay. Thanks. Let me know if you hear from her. I'll be home all day."

"Will do," she said. "You do the same. Leave a message if I don't pick up."

Samantha promised she would and then hung up, tapping the receiver with her finger. Kathy had to have gone somewhere. She didn't just disappear off the face of the earth.

Picking up the receiver again, she dialed Jeremy's number. Michael had said he hadn't seen her, but maybe Jeremy had and just didn't tell Michael. She hoped she got him and not anyone else who popped in and out of that house. Kathy said it was kind of like a revolving door with people coming and going all the time.

"Hello?"

"Jeremy?" Samantha asked, excited. It was the first time in her life she'd ever been happy to get him on the phone.

"Samantha?" He sounded confused.

"Yeah. Have you seen Kathy? I haven't heard from her since yesterday afternoon."

"Is she okay?"

"That's what I'm trying to figure out. I'm just checking in with different people. So, have you seen her?"

"Not in a couple weeks," he said. "She came by to get her stuff after we broke up at Paul's wake."

Samantha nodded. She didn't mean to be a reminder of his friend's death, but she also didn't want to not track down her sister because of an awkward encounter. "Okay. That's what I thought, but I figured I'd check anyway."

"If you find her, let me know," he said. "I'll check in with a few of our other friends too."

She smiled. Jeremy might be immature, but he wasn't a horrible person. He still cared about Kathy. "Thanks. I'll let you know when I find her."

Without even setting the phone back in its cradle, she pressed the switch hook and released it, waiting for a dial tone before she started punching in the number for the restaurant Kathy worked at. She was supposed to be working today and unless a major magical emergency came up—or if her boyfriend refused to take her, which she no longer had to worry about— Kathy always made her best effort to be at work.

A young woman's voice droned on the other end of the phone when she answered, spouting out the typical customer service greeting.

"Hi, this is Samantha Walker," she said after the woman finished her spiel. "I was wondering if I could talk to my sister Kathy."

"Hold on."

Samantha stared at the magic book on the table as she waited. She wasn't paying that close attention when Kathy read aloud about the valkyries yesterday morning, but from what she could remember, they had decided they were harmless. Were they wrong in that assumption? The book never usually had false information. Unless, it wasn't the valkyries who had Kathy, but something else entirely. And if that were the case, finding her would be nearly impossible without any further leads.

"Hello?" the young woman's voice said into the phone.

"Yes, I'm here."

"Yeah, Kathy didn't show up to work today."

"She didn't?" Samantha's heart beat faster.

"No and since this is her third strike, it's an automatic fire. So if you hear from her, she can come by and get her last check, but her termination is non-negotiable."

Samantha swallowed down the lump in her throat and tried to maintain a calm tone. "Okay. I'll tell her." She hung up quickly and wiped at her eyes as she moved to the book and flipped through the pages to find the entry on valkyries.

Kathy wasn't with Trisha.

She wasn't with Jeremy.

She didn't show up to work.

If the valkyries weren't the answer to this, Samantha would have to hunt down that guy Kathy met at the club. That would be her next best lead.

Finally, she landed on the entry on the valkyries and began to read. She was interrupted when the doorbell rang. All rational thought went out the window as relief washed over her. Kathy was home!

But the reality was, if it really was Kathy, she would've used her key instead of ringing the bell. Still, Samantha raced to the front door, hoping that it was somehow Kathy waiting on the other side.

CHAPTER 15

Eir and Tommy ended their tour of Valhalla at a balcony overlooking the arena. Together, they stared out below as the army the valkyries had assembled trained for Ragnarök.

There was a group of samurais dressed in full garb fighting with one another. In a different part of the arena, there were modern soldiers jumping on the sandy floor and crawling quickly under chicken wire before springing up and pointing their weapons at their other comrades. In yet a different corner were men dressed in full suits of armor swordfighting; the echoes of the metal clanging carrying up to the balcony.

"With your police background, we will place you in a group that plays to your strengths," Eir told Tommy. "Don't worry. We will take care to train you properly for Ragnarök, even if it is fast approaching."

He looked out and watched two swordsmen spar with one another. This was completely out of his wheelhouse. He never once considered himself a warrior. How did Eir expect him to fill that role so easily? Being a cop was completely different than fighting in a war. He was trained to de-escalate situations, not take as many lives as possible.

"You never told me how you knew I was a cop—police officer," Tommy said quietly. He slowly turned to her and added, "Before I…before I died."

"We have been watching you," Eir said. "We saw your true intentions behind your actions. You wore the badge not only with bravery and courage, but with compassion and kindness. Those are qualities we hope to see in the new world."

Tommy wondered how long he'd been watched. Did they know he was going to die? Did they know how he was going to die? He wished someone would've told him. He would've spent more time with his family. Been nicer to them. Hugged his daughter tighter, kissed his wife like he wouldn't ever see her again. If he had known the last times were his last times, they would've been different.

He felt a lump forming in his throat again and pushed the thoughts of his family away.

"But if this final battle is the end to the world as we know it, how will those qualities you saw in me carry through to the new world?" he asked. "Won't I be dead when the world is over?

Won't everyone be dead?"

"The world will not be over," she explained. "It will only be over as we know it and understand it today. Even we do not know what this new world will look like, but we can hope it will be one filled with compassion, strength, and love while limiting or eliminating the influences of evil and wrongdoing."

Tommy still looked confused. If the world ended, where did he go? That question would be better answered if he could wrap his head about where exactly he was now. Somewhere between living and dead. Like a ghost.

"But you, Thomas Wilson, you will persist," Eir explained. "Your time on Midgard has already come to an end. Your mission as a living person has been completed through your noble work as a policeman. Your mission as a spirit will be to help us bring about this new world by winning the war. After Ragnarök, your *afterlife* will begin, but your memories of when you were living will remain."

"So I'll remember what the world was like before the war?"

She nodded. "That is what we believe, yes. Keep in mind, this is all what we have deciphered through prophecies and other visions. However, it is my belief that those who are in the afterlife, the ones who remember what the world was like before Ragnarök, will be the ones to help maintain order in the new world. Life—in all of its forms—always has a purpose."

That made him feel a little better about dying so much sooner than he thought he would. But it still didn't reunite him with his family. It still didn't help his family understand the changes that were about to come. Would they know the world changed? Would they survive it? Was there going to be a complete exodus and rebirth to create the new world?

He had too many questions that didn't have answers. The best thing he could do not to overwhelm himself was to take it one step at a time. Looking out over the training warriors, he tried to find anyone who resembled a former police officer. That was harder to do in the mix of warriors from different countries and time periods.

"How do I fit in to this army?" he asked Eir.

"As we have discussed, you have certain qualities that—"

"No, I heard that." Tommy motioned out to the field. "I don't see any police officers out there. I see people who've been trained to kill people, not ones who have been trained to save them. If you said you've been recruiting *heroes* for centuries, then I can't be the first police officer to be recruited for this mission. There were certainly better police officers who came before me. Where are the rest of them?"

"Oh. I see." Eir nodded slightly and turned to look out at the training below. "Myself and the other valkyries have selected each one of these warriors carefully. In every one of these men and women, we saw that they were destined to be a part of something greater, even after their time in Midgard came to an end. The same can be said for you."

"But where are the cops?"

"Our job as valkyries is to understand the intricacies of the army we are creating. Its strengths and weaknesses. Finding heroes to become warriors that add to those strengths and eliminate those weaknesses as best as possible. Herja selected you because you will bring a set of skills our army needs. Skills that will meld perfectly with the other warriors in the army. The same can be said for the other police officers we have recruited."

"But where are they?" He was growing frustrated that his question wasn't being answered.

"In a special training area," she finally said. "Your background as a policeman means you have skills that will help our warriors take pause in moments of uncertainty. You will help guide our warriors to win the war by taking as few lives as possible. And when the war is over, you should have the option to be a part of shaping the new world order."

"Should?"

"As I have said, all of this is based in theory from prophecies and visions. It is the belief of the valkyries that heroes like policemen carry unique qualities that will help us beyond Ragnarök. There are other heroes who have been recruited that will not be a part of the war, but will assist with the rebuilding."

Tommy wondered who, exactly, but knew that Eir likely wouldn't answer that because it didn't concern him. He was just curious. What he needed to focus on was getting through to the afterlife so he could see his family again.

"Do you have anymore questions?" she asked.

"Not right now."

"Then follow me." She backed away from the banister and started toward the stairs. "I will introduce you to your new squad and you can begin your training."

CHAPTER 16

The benefit of being in the arena with the training warriors was that they were all so preoccupied with each other that none of them paid much attention to Kathy in her cage. It made her wonder how many times the valkyries had taken prisoners in the past. Although that went against what was alluded to in the magic book. Maybe the cage was meant for solitary confinement for a warrior gone rogue.

With the focus off of her, Kathy did what she could to find a way out of the cage. The bars were hard as a rock and the other walls, made of brick, didn't contain any weak points. Even using the bowl that came with her subpar dinner did nothing to deteriorate the structure.

Instead, Kathy used the bowl as a sort of shovel to dig into the sandy floor. She didn't know how far down it went, but that appeared to be the only option for escape.

"Attention everyone!" a woman's voice bellowed over the crowd.

Moments later, the arena was silenced and all the warriors turned to look up at Brynhildr standing on a balcony above the crowd.

Kathy slowed her shoveling to make sure no one noticed what she was up to. There were a number of valkyries moving around the arena, but none of them seemed to pay her any mind. Maybe she would get out of this cage after all. Getting home would be a whole different problem. But one thing at a time.

"It appears as though the impending battle of Ragnarök is coming much sooner than we anticipated," Brynhildr announced.

Throughout the arena, the warriors broke into chatter. This was the moment they'd been waiting for, and for some of them, they'd been waiting for centuries. The fact that it was now upon them was very exciting.

Kathy took advantage of the noise to dig even further. The deeper she got, the more sand she encountered. It appeared to be endless. Worse, she was running out of room in her cell to put it.

Several of the valkyries around the arena banged their weapons together. Another woman's voice from the other side of the arena called out, "Mind your voices while Brynhildr speaks!"

Slowly, the voices quieted to murmurs and then silenced altogether.

"As you are all aware, myself and the other valkyries have collected each one of your souls for the mission of fighting in the final battle against the enemies of the gods," Brynhildr continued. "Each and every time we have ventured into Midgard, we have maintained our stealth among those who dwell in the human world. However, two nights ago, one of our own was spotted."

More murmurs began again and Kathy realized that many of the warriors had turned their eyes to her. One of the valkyrie spears slapped hard against the bars on Kathy's cage.

"What do you think you are doing?" the valkyrie snapped at her. "Give me that if you ever want to have another meal again."

Kathy clutched the bowl to her chest. She didn't want to turn it over because it was her only way out of this cage. None of the valkyries seemed to be listening to reason.

"If you just hear me out, I'd be able to explain everything," Kathy said. "Ragnarök has not started! I don't have that kind of power!"

"That is exactly what the enemy would say so we will be caught by surprise." The valkyrie jabbed her spear toward Kathy. "Give me the plate or I will march you to Odin myself."

Reluctantly, Kathy handed over the plate. The valkyrie

stalked off out of sight, but nearly every single one of the warriors was looking at Kathy with hungry eyes. She kept to the back of her cage and slunk deeper into the hole she dug.

One by one, the warriors turned back to Brynhildr for her to continue addressing them.

"As you can see, we have managed to capture the woman who spotted us during the collection," she said. "Although we have made attempts to converse with the captive, she has refused to cooperate with us."

Kathy wanted to scream out that they hadn't made very many attempts. At least not without already considering her guilty in their minds. Hence, the cage. But looking out at the venomous crowd that had been training to be killers, she knew it was better to keep her mouth shut in the moment. She was very obviously vastly outnumbered.

"We will make additional attempts to try to figure out when exactly the final battle will begin," Brynhildr went on. "However, myself and the other valkyries wanted you all to know that Ragnarök is coming. You have all trained hard and well. Soon it will be time to put that training to the test. We will go over details with you at a later date once we have planned for them. In the meantime, I wish you all luck in your training. You are going to need it soon. Let that knowledge fuel you with vigor in the coming days."

The arena erupted in battle cries. Fists, many of them gripping weapons, were raised in the air as the arena dissembled into pandemonium before the warriors returned to their training.

As Brynhildr noted, there was a newfound energy buzzing around the arena. More battle cries shouted here and there as swords clanged, canons fired, and gunshots sounded.

Kathy turned inward and looked around her cage again, reassessing her options. If she thought she was short on options before, she was even worse off now that they took the only tool she had from her.

All that was left to try was magic, which she had avoided because she suspected that the valkyries would've been prepared for that. But the valkyries weren't magical. They weren't gods. They were servants of gods. Perhaps they didn't even have the power to contain a witch.

Resting her head against the brick wall with her feet in the hole she dug, Kathy closed her eyes and crafted a spell. If she could send a message to Samantha, something that would let her know where she was, maybe her sister could come with better preparations—and explanations—to save Kathy. That was the hope, at least.

Another hope was that Kathy would be able to use Samantha's new power growth to her advantage. Although she herself didn't have a mind specialty, Kathy figured she should be able to cast a spell that could project her, momentarily, into her sister's mind to communicate with her.

Casting a spell to return home would be useless. The

valkyries found Kathy once, they would do it again. Since they were training warriors, they might even bring reinforcements. And talking her way out of a recapture would be harder than talking herself out of her situation now. Better to call Samantha for help.

Once she had the spell crafted in her head, she held her fist to her chest and whispered it to herself, pushing all of her thoughts and energies to Samantha.

Blood connection to speak as one.
Connect me to someone I love.

The noises from the arena faded, as did the light pressing against her closed eyes. For a brief moment, Kathy watched as Samantha, through her own eyes, wrote on a pad of paper. At the top, "Valkyries" was scrawled, followed by a short bulleted list of facts about them, most of which was information they had obtained from *The Art of Magic*.

"Sam!" she called out.

Pain gripped Kathy's head and the noises of the arena sprung up again as she was pulled back to her cell. The spell must have backfired, even if there was a delay. The throbbing in Kathy's head, like a bad migraine, was enough for her to decide not to do it again. Apparently the valkyries had stronger containment charms on the cage than Kathy thought.

She only had a brief moment in Samantha's mind. She didn't

even get a chance to get her bearings, let alone give her sister a message. She only hoped that that moment in Samantha's mind was enough to let her sister know that something was wrong. Judging by what Samantha was working on, she had already figured out that Kathy was in trouble.

Hopefully she'd figure out where she was and how to save her too.

CHAPTER 17

Samantha was surprised when she opened the front door. "Steven! What are you doing here?"

"I came to talk," he said. "Can I come in?"

"Well…" Talk about horrible timing. On one hand, she was relieved that he came back and he wanted to talk things through—at least, she hoped that's why he came over—but on the other hand, she needed to find Kathy. Maybe even save her.

"I know you're probably mad for the way I reacted when you told me—when you told me you're a—"

"A witch?"

"Yeah." He offered a sad smile. "It was—I was surprised."

"I think 'mad' was more like it," she said. "And you were right. I shouldn't have kept such a big secret from you for so long. I'm sorry for that. As much as I'd love to talk, now isn't—"

"Just give me five minutes."

She studied him—grateful that she seemed to at least be grasping a small hold on her powers because his thoughts didn't immediately project into her mind.

Unless it wasn't really Steven.

Please let me in, please let me in, please let me in, she heard from his mind. *I hope I didn't mess up the best relationship I've ever had.*

Her heart melted with that thought and she stood aside and allowed him to enter.

"Thank you." He started to the living room. "Do you want to sit down?"

She turned and started back toward the kitchen. "You want to see a part of my world? Follow me."

Anxiety built inside her the closer they got to the kitchen, where she would reveal some of the details of her witchiness. Like the magic book. Or maybe he would get to see her craft a spell or a potion. Either way, his view into her world was about to get bigger.

"What's going on?" he asked.

"I think Kathy's in trouble," she explained as she retook her seat at the kitchen table in front of the book. "And I intend to find her."

"How do you know she's in trouble? Where is she? And what is that?" He sat beside her and looked over at the book.

"I haven't heard from her and neither have any of her friends. She didn't show up to work this morning, either."

"Well, that could just be Kathy being Kathy," he reasoned.

"Kathy can be a little irresponsible, yes, but she usually shows up when she says she's going to be somewhere," Samantha said. "Especially work. And honey, if you're going to be a part of my life completely, you need to be able to trust my gut on some of these things. Something's wrong."

"I take it we're not going to talk about us, then."

She grabbed his hands in hers and looked him in the eyes. "We need to. I want to. But I can't do that unless I know my sister's safe."

He nodded. "I suppose that's fair. Now what is this?"

Samantha got to her feet and retrieved a pad of paper and a pen from the junk drawer. "That's our family magic book. It's been passed down from generation to generation, being added to and modified as our family learns more about magic and the beings that exist beyond the nonmagical world."

"Beings?" *Ghosts.*

"Not just ghosts," Samantha said as she retook her seat. "And they're called spirits. Well, usually."

"Okay, what's going on? Can you read my mind?"

She scrunched her face. "Sort of, yeah."

"Sort of?"

"Our powers are rooted in a specialty," she explained. "My specialty is the mind. So the first iteration of that was to be able to use magic to persuade people. Apparently that's recently grown so now I can read minds too."

Great. Just what I want. A wife who knows exactly what I'm thinking.

Samantha couldn't help but smile at him. Steven was still thinking of how she was going to be his wife. The wedding wasn't off!

"They just recently grew," she told him. "I'm working on controlling it so I'll only able to read minds when I intend to. So be careful what you think until then."

Hopefully she doesn't find out that I had to take out a loan for her engagement ring. Or that I've already started talking to a realtor. Or that—

"Steven!" She brought her hands to her ears, as if that would stop her from reading his mind. "Think of something *other* than what you don't want me to know."

His face grew red. "Oh."

Setting the pad of paper beside the book, she wrote "Valkyries" at the top of the page and began listing all the details she knew for a fact about them.

"Valkyries?" Steven asked. "They're real?"

"Apparently."

Mr. Barrowhill told us about these in twelfth grade English class. Norse mythology, which was primarily in Scandinavia. Like the vikings—

"Steven, I'm sorry, but your thoughts are distracting *me*

from being able to think," Samantha said. "Maybe you should go—"

"*Sam!*"

She gripped Steven's arm and sat up straight.

"What is it?" he asked in a panic. "What's the matter? What's happening?"

"I heard Kathy's voice."

"You did?" He looked around, as if Kathy were hiding. "Where?"

"Shh!" She swatted at him to be quiet, then leaned forward on the table and closed her eyes. Putting her fingers to her temples, she tried to focus in on her new power and find Kathy's voice again.

Silence.

"Damn it!" She slapped her hand on the table. "I swear I heard her call my name."

"Maybe you just wanted to hear—"

"*No,*" she said firmly to him. "I told you, my gut is telling me that something is wrong. And this power may be new, but I know what I heard. It was my sister."

"And you think the valkyries are responsible?" he asked in disbelief. "They don't even have any enemies! They're gods or something."

"No matter what they are, they're my best lead to finding my sister."

"How?"

"She saw one! Now, I'm sorry, but since you don't have magic and I don't have time to explain everything I'm doing, I think it's best if you go home and we talk later. I'm not trying to push you off, but I need to focus all of my energy on Kathy."

Sounds like you're pushing me off. He rose to his feet and started to the door. "Fine. Call me when she's safe." *Sounds to me like this is all blown way out of proportion. If the valkyries are real, then so is Valhalla and Asgard.*

"Asgard," Samantha murmured to herself. She jumped up and raced to follow Steven to the door. "Wait, I have a question."

Now she wants to talk.

She pointed to the floor. "This world is Midgard, right?" Samantha knew the answer from what the book said, but she was testing his knowledge on the subject, as well as his reliability.

"In Norse *mythology*, yes." He crossed his arms. "Why?"

"So that would make the world where the gods live…"

"Asgard. Samantha, you're not seriously thinking this is real, right?"

"I have to," she said. "There's a suspension of disbelief that needs to happen when you're a witch. Anything is possible and we need to consider all options. Now, one last question: if Valhalla were real, it would be in Asgard, right?"

"I don't remember the specifics." He shrugged. "Probably, yeah."

She smiled and patted him on the arm. "Thanks! You've

been a big help!" As she turned to leave, he called out to her.

"So does this mean I can stay?"

"No, sorry!" she said from the back of the house. "I'll call you after I find her. Thanks again! Love you!"

Back in the kitchen, Samantha sat at the table and reached for the pad of paper. She ripped off the sheet she'd written on and started crafting a spell to transport her to her sister.

She had no idea what to expect in Asgard or where to find Valhalla. But she didn't have time to run to the library to research the mythology. Not to mention, all the thoughts of all the people downtown would give her a headache and she wouldn't be able to think.

Crossing off another couplet that didn't quite work, Samantha started another. The wording needed to be perfect, but the truth was, Samantha was never very good at crafting spells. That was always the area that Kathy excelled at.

Too bad Kathy was the one she needed the spell for.

CHAPTER 18

Samantha spent longer than she intended to writing the spell to take her to Valhalla. Not only did spell crafting not come easy to her, but she also wanted to combine it with the strength of some herbs and strategically-colored candles to give the spell a little more *oomph*.

While herbs and making potions were among the things she was confident in as a witch, it still required research within *The Art of Magic* and other books about making potions. And research took time. Time that Kathy might not have.

As much as Samantha wanted to believe in what the book said—and what Steven said—about the valkyries not being vengeful people, her intuition was telling her otherwise. Not to mention, she knew for a fact that she heard Kathy call out her name. That much was proof to her that her intuition was right. Or at least on the right track.

Finally, after Samantha had ground up bits of comfrey and feverfew, both to assist her while she traveled, and mixed them together, she sprinkled the herbs on a tray and placed a silver candle in the center of it before lighting it. Silver was supposed to represent neutrality in this spell, which she hoped would help send the message that she wasn't invading their world with bad intentions. She only wanted to reconnect with her sister.

Holding the spell up, she breathed in a deep breath before reciting:

Changing winds and changing tides,
Show me where my sister hides.
Through all worlds and through all stars,
Let us reconnect our hearts.

The air in the room swirled, blowing out the flame on the candle. Samantha's vision was filled with bright light and she blinked against its harshness. When she opened them again, she was suddenly outside, feeling a cool refreshing breeze against her skin.

Blue skies and fluffy clouds filled the space around her, as if she were standing among the clouds. Below her feet, she stood on something that had the colors of a rainbow. As she stepped closer to one side, she noticed it was a bridge. Looking back, she saw that the opposite end behind her stretched on for a long time, disappearing into the clouds. She turned to look forward and stumbled backward at what she saw.

Standing in front of a brick wall with tall wooden double doors leading inside was a man even taller than the wall he protected. In one hand, he had a large sword. In another, he held a long, skinny horn.

Was this where Kathy was? Samantha saw no sign of her and it wasn't like there was anywhere for her to hide. She must be inside the protective wall, which meant that this was Asgard. Of course, that was assuming that Samantha was right about the valkyries taking Kathy. That meant that somewhere inside Asgard was Valhalla and somewhere inside *that* was her sister.

A long shot, but the only shot she had.

The tall man grunted and stepped forward, the rainbow bridge shaking with each step. Samantha feared that it would crumble beneath them. He had a mean look and he raised his sword for an attack.

Samantha held her ground, but wondered if she was already as good as dead.

CHAPTER 19

Kathy's head was still throbbing later that day after the warriors had left the arena. In their wake, several valkyries lingered. They returned weapons to the armory, smoothed out the sand from the day's training, and by the end of the chores, they stood in a group talking. They were too far away for Kathy to hear what they were discussing, but she wondered if it was about her or Ragnarök. Then again, to them, those topics were one in the same.

Despite her own growing hunger, she didn't dare ask any of the valkyries for something else to eat. If she had any chance of getting out of here, she needed to be the willing, accommodating, *kind* prisoner. If the valkyries didn't see a threat in her, maybe they would start to question if she really was the sign of the beginning of Ragnarök.

Slim chance, but it was all she had at this point. She'd tried everything else.

Kathy had pushed most of the sand back into the hole she'd dug. It was dumb of her to think that she'd be able to dig her way out, but if she was honest with herself, she would consider trying it again. She was getting desperate. But her latest plan to seem as defenseless as possible to the valkyries would take time and concentration. That required her to cover up her previous attempts at escape.

One of the valkyries appeared on the other side of the bars of the cage and scared Kathy at her sudden appearance. The sandy floor prevented footsteps from being heard.

"Sorry," the valkyrie said. "I thought you could use something to eat." She passed Kathy a bowl filled with an assortment of food: an apple, hazelnuts, wild mushrooms, and even a small bit of what smelled like steaming fish.

Kathy took it and gave the fish a curious look.

"I cooked it myself," she said. "You do not have to worry about getting sick."

The witch looked up and realized that the valkyrie was the one she saw back in Erie. The one who started all of this. Herja.

"Thank you," Kathy said. "Do you mind if I ask you some questions? I haven't been able to get anyone to talk to me."

Herja looked back at the group of valkyries who had been talking nearby. The number in the group had dwindled and they were dispersing. For the most part, the arena was empty.

"Yes, I suppose that is okay."

"Thank you." Kathy reached into the bowl for the nuts. If nothing else, they would keep her full for longer. She had no idea when her next meal would be and this was already heartier than the bread and cheese she got when she arrived.

"The truth is," Herja started, "when I saw you the night I collected Thomas Wilson's soul, I saw the virtue in *your* soul as well. I know that you attempted to save him before I arrived. Even when I showed up, you wanted to make sure he would be taken care of in his death."

"Yes! That's exactly what happened!" Kathy said with excitement. She was so happy that someone was finally acknowledging her side of the story. "But why did you attack me? If you knew I meant well?"

Herja knelt on the sand just outside the bars. "I was scared. No one on Midgard had ever seen a valkyrie unless we allowed ourselves to be seen. But you did. How?"

"Well, I'm a witch."

Herja shook her head. "We have collected souls in front of witches before. Many times. None of them have seen us. What was different about our encounter?"

Kathy picked at more of the food in the bowl, pulling away pieces of the fish and eating it little by little. "Well, I was, uh…drunk."

"Drunk?" Herja asked, confused.

"Intoxicated? Inebriated? Under the influence?"

The valkyrie's face was still contorted in confusion. "Under the influence…of evil?"

"No!" Kathy said quickly. "You know, alcohol. It lowers your inhibitions if you have too much. Changes your state of mind."

"Oh! I see! Our master, Odin, gained his knowledge by drinking from Mimic's well, which contains dew from the roots of Yggdrasil, the Tree of Life."

Kathy nodded slowly. The state she was in the other night was not nearly as noble as gaining knowledge from an ancient, mythical tree, but she didn't correct the valkyrie. Not when they were finally making progress.

"Some of the gods drink wine and mead, but as valkyries we are not allowed," Herja continued.

"How come?"

"We need to always be prepared for war."

"You don't ever get a night off?"

Herja shook her head. "We need to stay clear-headed and focused in case Heimdall gives the sound."

"Heimdall?"

"The guardian of Asgard," she explained. "He watches over the bridge of Bifröst for intruders or if Loki ever escapes from his containment."

Kathy nodded slowly. It all sounded like a foreign language to her, but Herja continued to show her kindness so Kathy just sat and listened. "I see."

"So you think you only saw me by accident?"

Kathy nodded. "I didn't even know valkyries existed. I think it was just an aligning of several coincidences that created the perfect atmosphere for me to see you. I never meant to interfere with your mission. Actually, I was talking to my sister right before you guys brought me here. We decided that you guys were harmless and we didn't need to get involved."

Herja looked concerned. "You told someone else about us?"

"Just my sister." That did nothing to pacify the valkyrie. "She's not going to tell anyone else."

"That is cause for concern." Herja looked around the arena for another valkyrie.

Kathy shook her head frantically. "No, Samantha won't tell anyone! Your secret is safe."

"We cannot take that risk."

"But you even said yourself that you saw the virtue in me, right?" Kathy pleaded. "You know I'm telling the truth when I say that I don't mean you guys any harm."

Herja narrowed her eyes. "Yes. But for your sister, I cannot be sure. Besides, we make decisions together as valkyries. Brynhildr has already alerted the army that Ragnarök has started. The wheels are in motion."

"But it hasn't started! Look, you think that me seeing you the other night is a sign that things are changing, right?"

Herja nodded.

"So make your case to the other valkyries. Let them see for

themselves that I'm not a threat to you."

She shook her head. "I am not sure they will agree."

Kathy chewed on her bottom lip as she racked her brain for another idea. "You said that Odin is your master, right? Does he trump every decision the valkyries make?"

"I suppose you could say that," Herja said. "The issue has never come up before. On occasion."

"Let me talk to him and plead my case," Kathy offered. "If he can see the good in me, then the other valkyries will have to agree as well."

"I am not sure I can allow that."

"Herja, please. I'm begging you. I don't belong here. I belong back home protecting the nonmagical from the supernatural. That's my job as a witch. Let me go and you can go back to doing your job as a valkyrie."

Herja studied her. "You make a good case."

"Because you know I'm right! If I can just talk to Odin, I know I can get him to understand that I saw you by accident. I'm not the sign you've been waiting for. Ragnarök is not beginning!"

Again, Herja considered this. Finally, she admitted, "It has been prophesied that the start of Ragnarök would begin with the sound of Heimdall's horn, signaling the escape of Loki from his containment."

"And if Loki hasn't escaped, there's no threat to fight," Kathy said. "Herja, you have to help me. You're my only hope of getting out of here."

The valkyrie once again looked around the arena. "The warriors are returning from their meal. I will consider your request. But do not speak a word of this to anyone."

CHAPTER 20

The tall man swung his sword at Samantha. She jumped back in time, but felt the rush of air pass over her legs as it just barely missed her.

Do not chase her, his thoughts said in her head. *If she retreats, I will still have done my job.*

Samantha watched the man and waited for him to say something. It was one thing to annoy Kathy or Steven with her mind reading, but it was an entirely different thing to do that to some mythical guardian.

She is not leaving. I should sound the alarm.

The man raised the horn in his other hand and brought it to his lips.

"Wait!" Samantha cried out. "Don't do anything until you

hear me out!"

There was no telling who he would be calling if she let him sound the horn. Or worse, what kind of chaos she'd encounter whenever she figured out how to get inside the walls of Asgard.

Slowly, the man lowered the horn and motioned for her to plead her case. *Lets see what she has to say.*

"I'm a witch from, uh…Midgard," she started. "I don't mean to intrude, but the valkyries took my sister and I'm just here to free her and take her back home, where we will never bother you guys again." She pushed her persuasion toward him and added, "I don't mean you or the citizens of Asgard any harm. I'm only here for my sister."

She is not a threat—

But what if she is lying?

I can let her pass through, she seems harmless enough—

But what if this is the threat I have been tasked with stopping?

Samantha listened as contradicting thoughts played out in his mind. Her persuasion wasn't working the way she'd hoped it would. Using more energy, she tried again. "We are good witches. We fight evil. Supernatural evil, that is. We're like you guys up here in Asgard. Protecting the world order. The valkyries are just mistaken about my sister. She is just like me! Good."

She is good—

Unless the witch has cast a spell?

Unless I am under a hex that I cannot see.

I should sound the alarm since I cannot be certain I am not in the right state to make this decision. This woman could be the end to us all and I would be the first to fall.

"Wait!" Samantha called out, pushing her persuasion again.

The man stopped with the hand holding the horn frozen halfway up to his mouth. He stared at her with wide eyes, awaiting his next command.

Nothing like the present to practice controlling her new power. Focusing her energy on projecting into his mind, Samantha pushed good thoughts at him.

I only came to get my sister, she told him with her thoughts. *I don't want to cause anyone harm. I'm not here on the orders of any enemies. I just want to take my sister home.*

The man's expression softened as her magic took hold. She hoped that it was working, but focused her concentration on maintaining the connection until he let her in.

The more she pushed, the more of his thoughts she saw. Like his own name, Heimdall. Or the thought of an older man—Odin, she read from his thoughts—wearing a fur-lined coat and riding a majestic horse with eight legs—Sleipnir—appointing him to guard Asgard because he was unable to speak. She also saw a valkyrie bringing a man across Bifröst and through the gate into Asgard. Another thought was of the same valkyrie, with two others dragging Kathy into Asgard.

At least that confirmed that her sister was here, but until Samantha got herself inside, it put her no further ahead.

If you let me in, the citizens of Asgard will remain safe, she pushed into Heimdall's mind some more. *The only one I am here for is my sister.*

Another one of Heimdall's thoughts popped into her mind: the layout of Asgard. It wasn't anything concrete, but she very clearly saw the route—through memories of landmarks and streets—from the gate of Asgard to the steps of Valhalla. If she ever got inside, she wouldn't have a problem finding the hall the valkyries called home.

I believe my sister is being held against her will, Samantha continued. *The valkyries took her because they fear her, but there's nothing to fear. Help me right a wrong committed by your people!*

That seemed to do the trick. Heimdall straightened up and shook his head, as if to clear Samantha away from his mind. He gave her a curt nod and then reached behind him to pull on the door handle of the gate.

With a grunt, he pulled the door open and motioned for Samantha to enter.

Cautiously, she stepped by him and through the gate into the citadel of Asgard. She only hoped that she wasn't stepping into a deathtrap.

CHAPTER 21

There was a buzz of energy in Valhalla as the warriors gathered for another meeting regarding Ragnarök. Tommy stood in the back among the other police heroes who made up the army. It had only been a short training session so far, but they seemed nice enough. Most of all, they were patient with Tommy and his adjustment to his new life.

Beside the police officers was a group of rowdy swordsmen who seemed to not spare a second of training time. They continued to spar with one another until a valkyrie's voice boomed out and called for attention.

Nearly instantly, the energized army in the Hall of the Slain fell into order with full attention on the balcony to hear the valkyrie speak.

"We will begin our meeting about preparations for Ragnarök," she said, which brought cheers and battle cries.

"Who is that?" Tommy asked the policewoman standing beside him as the crowd cheered around them.

"Brynhildr," she said.

"Is she the leader?"

"Not exactly. The valkyries don't have any one leader specifically, but Brynhildr is the one who takes charge most of the time."

Tommy nodded.

To regain order, Brynhildr raised her fist and waited, tight-lipped until the arena quieted again and she continued her speech. "While the alarm has not officially sounded yet, we have reason to believe that the battle is imminent. Possibly even as early as tomorrow we will march against Loki and the giants."

The buzz of excitement exploded. There were smiles on everyone's faces, cheering and whooping and throwing fists in the air.

Once again, Brynhildr held her fist up to quiet the room. When she had everyone's attention again, she continued. "As you have been trained and have come to understand, this battle will be fierce. It will result in many of you moving on to the afterlife in a way that none of us have planned—painfully and gruesomely. But no matter what, your spirits *will move on*. That is not to mean that you should not fight your hardest. Each of you have been hand-picked through the centuries because of your courage, passion, and skill. Do not lose those qualities in times of war. We are fighting for something bigger than the lives you lived on Midgard, even bigger than the lives we live here on Asgard. We are about to change the world."

Another eruption of battle cries ensued. Tommy felt guilty because he didn't share the excitement. As much as everyone he encountered tried to help him adjust, tried to help him feel welcome, the fact of the matter was that he didn't want to be here in Valhalla, or Asgard. He wanted to be back in his old life with his family.

But whining and complaining and dragging his feet was not going to return him to his old life. There was no going back. Only going forward. He once prided himself on the fact that he so frequently made his family proud simply by going to work every day and doing his job—helping strangers while supporting his family.

Now in this new world, he had a new destiny. Something he still hadn't fully wrapped his head around yet. But just like he did when he was with them, he was going to do his best to fulfill his new destiny to make his family proud, even if it would be years and years before they joined him in the afterlife.

The hardest part for Tommy was that he wouldn't be able to come home to his family for support to keep him going on during the days he felt like giving up. He would have to keep them in his memory and think of them when things got hard, as it sounded like they were about to be.

"…we will need artillery to take out the giants," Brynhildr said. "And that artillery will need warriors to protect the giants from—"

The crowd began to murmur, growing in volume, as several valkyries ran off to the side of the arena opposite the armory. Everyone had their theories and nobody was shy about sharing them.

"What's going on?" Tommy asked one of the former officers beside him.

"I don't know," he said.

"There's someone in here," one of the swordsman said loudly to no one in particular. "The alarm hasn't been sounded, but she said before that Ragnarök is starting in a way that's different than we all thought."

"Are you saying we're being ambushed?" another warrior asked.

The swordsman put up his hands. "I'm not saying anything one way or another. All I'm saying is there's possibilities."

"I think there's someone in here," the police officer told Tommy. "Maybe not necessarily an enemy, but someone who's not normally here."

As the crowd began to get more restless, Tommy's heart beat faster. He tried his best to prepare himself for what was about to happen, but the truth of the matter was that he felt woefully unprepared and as a former police officer, he liked to know what was most likely about to happen next.

CHAPTER 22

Samantha walked through the streets of Asgard with purpose. Her clothes didn't resemble any of the gods and demigods on the street she passed and she knew for a fact that she was being watched. The sooner she got to Valhalla, the better. Hopefully she and Kathy would be able to make a clean getaway too.

Using the memories she got from Heimdall's mind, she navigated the tight, winding streets until she came upon a large marble hall with stone pillars and timber supports.

Valhalla.

Hurrying around to the side, she found a door and slowly stepped inside. In a building full of trained warriors, she was anticipating some sort of resistance. But to her surprise, the hall she stepped into was fairly quiet.

Samantha followed the long corridor down the length of the structure. She rounded a corner, looking for an exit out of the hallway that would lead her anywhere. Heimdall's memories didn't recall being inside Valhalla so she was completely on her own.

From the end of the next hallway, Samantha spotted a valkyrie appear from around the corner.

"Who are you?" the valkyrie demanded. "Intruder!"

Samantha looked around for an escape, didn't see one, and started to turn to run back the way she came. But the valkyrie was faster, reaching her before Samantha had a chance to get very far.

The valkyrie whacked Samantha hard on the side with her spear and the witch struggled to try to get control of it. The valkyrie was swift and swung the spear around to deliver another blow, but Samantha caught it and gripped the handle of the spear while she drove a foot into the valkyrie's stomach.

"I'm not here to hurt anyone," she said, noting the irony that she just kicked this woman.

The valkyrie ignored her and came at Samantha with a raised fist, meanwhile loosening her grip on the spear. Samantha took advantage and swung the spear around, whacking the valkyrie in her side before pointing the sharp edge at her and taking a step back. They had rotated, so now Samantha's back was to the direction the valkyrie had come from.

"Don't move," the witch said. She tried to use the same game she did with Heimdall. Push her new telepathic abilities into the valkyrie's mind to get her to let her pass. But there was resistance. Almost like a shield that prevented Samantha from penetrating her mind.

"I'm not going to hurt anyone," Samantha said, this time using her persuasion. "I'm just here to get my sister and leave."

The persuasion had no effect and the valkyrie took a step toward her. So Samantha tried to invade her mind again as it seemed to have at least *some* effect.

The valkyrie's shoulders slumped and her face went blank. Although Samantha was unable to penetrate her mind, she still seemed to have at least managed to confuse her. Hopefully that would be enough to make an escape.

Samantha tried to throw a few more disarming thoughts at the valkyrie, but quickly dropped the spear and ran around the next corner, where a tall staircase led her up to the sound of cheering and roaring.

Stepping into the vast arena full of warriors of all backgrounds, Samantha watched for a moment as they all held their attention on a valkyrie speaking from up on a balcony overlooking the arena. From the sound of it, she was encouraging them to fight. To keep morale in battle.

The eavesdropping came to a quick end when Samantha noticed several warriors spot her waiting in the doorway.

Worse, she could see valkyries wind their way through the crowd toward her.

Stepping into the arena, Samantha was surprised to feel that the floor was sandy. It probably helped warriors train for agility.

She kept close to the outer wall and moved along it, seeing another doorway underneath the balcony. It would be risky to get there with the crowd in the arena facing that direction, but if Kathy were being held anywhere it'd be—

Right here! There were several cages tucked in along the outer wall of the arena. In the third one down sat her sister on the sandy floor.

"Kathy?" Samantha nearly shrieked.

"Sam!" Kathy hugged her sister through the bars. "How did you find me?"

"Long story," she said. "But your message helped."

"So I *did* get through to you!"

Samantha nodded and smiled.

"Watch out!" Kathy screamed and looked behind her sister.

Samantha just barely registered that the valkyrie on the balcony had stopped talking and the arena had erupted into murmurs. Two seconds later, she felt multiple hands on her as she was ripped away from Kathy's cage and pinned to the sandy floor.

"Hey! Wait!" Samantha cried out. "I'm only here to get my sister and bring her home! I'm not here to hurt you!"

"That is the one!" The valkyrie Samantha had confused in

the hallway stood clutching her side, pointing an accusatory finger at Samantha. "She attacked me!"

"I did not!" Samantha shouted, but the valkyries didn't listen. They opened the door to the cage beside Kathy and threw Samantha inside.

"Your own judgement will come," the valkyrie said.

The warriors in the arena erupted into cheers once the door to Samantha's cage was sealed shut.

The valkyrie on the balcony raised her fist and the room quieted.

"Heroes! It seems the other valkyries and myself have some business to take care of," she said. "We will continue announcing our plans for Ragnarök at another time. Until then, rest up. We have big days ahead of us."

The warriors again shouted out in roars and battle cries. Fists flew into the air as they marched across the arena and through the doors that Samantha had originally intended to scope out.

Instead, she sat trapped in her cage as she watched the vast amount of warriors disappear out of the arena, kicking up sand in their wake. All except one. A man who appeared to be about Samantha's age. He stopped and stared in the direction of the sisters' cages.

Samantha thought that maybe this was a chance for rescue. Maybe he would tell the valkyries how wrong it was to put them in cages. How they should be set free.

Another valkyrie approached him. One with a kinder face.

"Thomas, why are you not following the others?"

He looked over at Kathy's cage and met her eyes.

"Is something the matter?" the valkyrie asked him, putting a gentle hand on his shoulder.

The man looked around and noticed several valkyries watching him. He muttered an apology to the kind valkyrie and jogged to catch up with the rest of the warriors.

As he left the arena, so did Samantha's hope of getting out of the cage anytime soon.

CHAPTER 23

"Sam? Are you awake?" Kathy asked quietly. Despite whispering, her voice echoed across the vast arena. She leaned against the brick wall and sat as close to the bars of the cage as possible in an effort to get as close to her sister as she could.

"Yeah." From the sound of Samantha's voice, it seemed to Kathy that her sister was sitting in a similar position as she was. "Can't sleep. If we're going to break out of here, now's the time to do it. When everyone's asleep."

The valkyries had given them something to eat for dinner—more bread and cheese. Kathy figured that Samantha's arrival upset the valkyries enough not to give them a more substantial meal. After their food was delivered and their dishes retrieved, the valkyries left the witches alone in the arena. Shortly after, the sunlight faded and darkness took over.

"I tried," Kathy said. "There's no way out. Notice how they took our dishes? They don't even want us to use them as tools to get out of here."

"What about a spell?" Samantha asked. "You got a message to me before."

"And my head is still pounding from the backfire." Kathy rubbed her forehead.

"So what do you think we should do? I'm not just going to sit here."

"We're out of all other options. Besides, I think at least some of the valkyries might be coming around to the idea that I'm not lying. One of them brought me a pretty substantial lunch and actually talked to me. Hopefully that won't all be messed up from you showing up like you did."

"Sorry for trying to save you," Samantha said.

"Sam, I'm not yelling at you," Kathy said. "I'm just saying, maybe the valkyries are realizing that Ragnarök is not starting after all."

"Correct me if I'm wrong, but do they think that *you* are the sign that this final battle is starting?"

"That sounds about right. I think they're all just so hyped up about it because they've been waiting for this battle for a few centuries, judging by the people in their army."

"I noticed that," Samantha said. "It's like taking a trip

through the past. It's weird."

"I don't care about their army, as long as they don't come for us. I just want to get home."

Samantha let out a heavy sigh. "Me too."

"Did something happen?" Kathy picked up on something in her sister's tone.

"What do you mean?"

"Well, first of all you're kind of grumpy. And second, you seem to be itching to get home for something bigger than safety. Spill." Kathy circled her finger in the sand as she waited for her sister to respond. The sand was decently comfortable, but she couldn't wait to get back to solid floors again.

"Steven came to the house this morning," Samantha started. "Before I cast the spell to come here."

"That's good, though, right?"

"Yeah," Samantha said in a tone that gave the impression that it wasn't good news.

"What? Did he not want to talk to you about being a witch?"

"No, he did. But I was so worried about you that I let him talk while I did some more digging into the valkyries."

Kathy wanted to ask if Samantha had found out anything they didn't already know, but she knew Samantha needed to talk about Steven first.

"Actually," Samantha went on, "thanks to this new power, I picked up what he remembered about valkyries from high school."

"You didn't tell him that, did you?"

"Well, I didn't want to lie to him," Samantha said. "But it was good because he helped me figure out where you were. Of course, I pretty much kicked him out the door because I wanted to come find you."

"I'm sure he'll understand," Kathy said. "Now that he knows you're a witch, you don't have to lie to him. That's gotta count for something."

"Yeah."

"And it's a good sign that he came to you on his own to talk things over." Kathy thought about Jeremy and how he wouldn't have come to talk things through with her. He wouldn't even realize they were going through a rough patch if she didn't point it out. But that was all behind her now. She and Jeremy were broken up. Time to move forward and look to the future.

"That's a sign that he's willing to work through the rough patch," she said. "Because that's all this is, Sam. A rough patch. You two will get through this."

"I hope so. I just hope that I didn't push him away by blowing him off."

"I really don't think it's that big of a deal," Kathy said. "Besides, he's going to have to get used to it once you guys are married."

Samantha didn't say anything and Kathy wondered if she touched a nerve by mentioning the wedding. The way Samantha was upset after she told Steven her secret, Kathy thought that there might not be a wedding. And even though Steven showing up to talk things over was a good sign, it didn't mean he was ready to jump back into wedding plans and walk down the aisle with Samantha.

Kathy kicked herself for bringing it up, but before she had a chance to apologize, Samantha changed the subject.

"Another casualty to this whole valkyrie thing is that you were supposed to work today—or yesterday. It's hard to keep track of time here."

"Strike three," Kathy said. "Automatic fire. The 'no excuses' policy."

"Kathy, I'm sorry."

She shrugged, even though Samantha couldn't see it. "Meh, it's okay. I didn't even like that job anyway. I was just there because it was better than having no job. Guess it's back to the want ads."

"This could actually turn into an opportunity for you."

"To find a better job? Yeah. Definitely nothing in food service. Maybe a clothing store—although that could get dangerous. I wonder if there's anything at the mall. But then, the bus routes out there are still iffy. Better to find something downtown so I can travel easier."

"No, Kathy, I meant this could be an opportunity to stick to that plan we agreed on when I graduated high school."

Kathy thought about that plan. They agreed that they'd both pay for not only the bills with the house, but for Samantha to go to college. Once Samantha graduated and got a better-paying job, it would be Kathy's turn to go to college.

But that had been years ago. Kathy wasn't sure she even wanted to go to college anymore. So instead she played dumb. "What plan?"

"The one you were just thinking of!" Samantha said.

"Okay, we need to talk about this whole mind-reading thing," Kathy said. "New rule: you don't read my mind unless it's absolutely necessary. And even then, I want you to hesitate."

"I can't exactly help it right now," Samantha said.

"Well try. It's creepy the way you're fishing around in my mind like that and I don't even know."

"Okay, okay," Samantha said. "I'll back off. But can we get back to the plan?"

"That was a long time ago." Kathy didn't like to think about her last few years of high school. Their dad abandoned them her junior year, which forced them to both get jobs to pay the bills.

It wasn't fun and it wasn't easy, all on top of dealing with the fact that their father—who they had otherwise had a decent relationship with, being that he was their only parent—had walked out on them without a trace.

The sisters made that pact as a survival mechanism that Kathy didn't think they needed anymore. It was a goal they had set to get them out of the lowest point of their lives.

Now they had figured things out. Samantha had made it through college and gotten a job she liked. She was supporting them and Kathy was helping with her part-time work. Besides, it worked for them because they also had responsibilities as witches. Changing that dynamic created a future that Kathy couldn't quite picture. And that scared her a bit.

"So?"

"I don't know, Sam."

"You would have to go part-time," Samantha said. "So it'll take longer, but that might be easier as far as scheduling goes. And the workload would be lighter. Have you given any thought as to what you might want to do?"

"Mmm, not really."

"That's okay!" Samantha beamed, clearly much more excited than Kathy was. "You can go and get your gen-eds done and decide in another year or two. Talk to a school counselor or something. They should be able to help."

"Are you sure that's something we can even afford?" Kathy asked, fishing for an excuse.

"We'll make it work. Kathy, I feel bad that you made sacrifices for me to get my feet on the ground, so I'm willing to make sacrifices for you to have a fair start too. We've had some bad luck the last couple years, but we're coming through on the other side now."

Kathy admired the fact that her sister wanted to help so badly. And it was true, Kathy did put her future on hold for Samantha to secure hers. But Kathy never really saw herself in college anyway. It didn't seem like a sacrifice.

"I guess it is the responsible thing to do," Kathy admitted. "But isn't it too late to sign up for the fall semester? I mean, it's already the middle of August. Don't classes start in another week or two?"

"It doesn't hurt to ask! And with some colleges, you can sign up the first day of classes. With gen-eds, you have a better chance of being able to just walk up."

"Sam, there isn't a community college in Erie, so where would I even take classes? I wouldn't want to go to an expensive school just for gen-eds."

"There's Porreco College. It's through Edinboro University. It's new, but it's essentially like a community college."

"You've done some research on this, haven't you?"

"Kathy, this has been the plan since *my* first day of classes," she said. "I want to make sure you're taken care of for the future. I think Porreco would be a good start for you."

Kathy sighed. "Okay, I'll think about it. But let's not forget, all of this hinges on us getting out of here. I can't take classes if we're dead."

"True, but I think—"

The sound of a slamming door stopped Samantha mid-sentence. Three valkyries stepped into the arena and walked directly toward their cages. Brynhildr led Eir and Herja with a stern look. Following close behind them was the man from the alley. The one who stopped and looked at Kathy earlier when the other warriors marched out of the arena.

CHAPTER 24

"Samantha! Open up!" Steven knocked on the door again to the Walker house. When no answer came, he tried to peek through the stained glass windows, but the house was dark. He couldn't see anything.

Another knock. "Samantha! Kathy! I hope you're both okay."

Stepping back, he looked up to the second floor windows. There weren't any lights on inside from what he could tell.

Where could they be? he wondered. He checked his watch. It was going on ten o'clock now.

Asgard.

Samantha said there was a misunderstanding with some valkyries and that she thought Kathy was in Asgard. But that wasn't real? Was it?

At the moment, Steven was having a hard time wrapping his head around what was real and what wasn't. He liked concrete answers—part of the reason why he made a good accountant—but this world that Samantha exposed him to contained all kinds of uncertainties. And that didn't sit right with him, especially because the woman he cared most about in the world was at the center of it all.

"Sam, come on, I just want to talk to you about…everything." It was his last-ditch effort. The one to try to convince himself that Samantha just went to bed early and that Kathy was probably out at a club somewhere.

But just like Samantha was telling him earlier about her intuition, Steven felt something in *his* gut that told him that everything was *not* okay with the girls.

Stepping off the front porch, he followed the driveway alongside the house to the back door. He fished for the key Samantha had made for him—back door only so the neighbors didn't think he was an intruder—and let himself into the kitchen.

The first thing he noticed was that the lights were off. The next thing was the mess on the floor—some dried green powder that had a rich scent to it—and a candle sitting on a plate on the table. Luckily, it was no longer lit, but the relief didn't last long.

"Samantha?" Steven's voice had a faint quiver to it as he moved through the house, checking each of the rooms. He was terrified of what he might find. If the valkyries were real—and

Samantha was sure that they were—then what other kind of bad things were out there that would want to hurt her?

The dining room was clear. So was the living room. He slowly made his way up the stairs, cringing each time the floors creaked. It was something he thought gave the house character before. Now he worried that character might be the death of him if it gave away his location to an intruder.

On the landing at the top of the stairs, he slowly peeked into each of the bedrooms, checking closets and under each bed, but didn't see anything. He noticed the door leading up to the attic, but decided not to check it out. There was no way the sisters would be up there.

Steven started to descend the stairs, but stopped halfway. What if the girls *were* in the attic?

Turning around, he went back up and slowly opened the attic door, climbing stairs that creaked even louder from disuse. Other than a lot of dust and cobwebs, there was nothing on the top floor of the house.

"Where are you, Samantha?" Steven muttered to himself. He gave half a mind to calling the police, but knew that there wasn't much they could do for him in this situation. If something did happen to Samantha, it was witch-related. Even if it wasn't, it hadn't been a full twenty-four hours since Samantha had last been spotted. He didn't think he could fill out a missing persons report yet.

With that option eliminated, he turned and went back

down to the first floor.

As he walked in the kitchen, he noticed something he had missed before when he first entered. Sitting on the kitchen table where Samantha had it when he stopped over earlier, the large book she had been reading sat spread open.

Glancing at the page, he read the entry on valkyries. Once again, he looked over at the mess on the island and the one lone candle. Beside the candle was a note. Four lines, all rhymes.

A spell.

She was gone.

"Samantha, what did you get yourself into?"

CHAPTER 25

Samantha stood when the valkyries approached with the man. The valkyrie with the stern look—the one who had been speaking on the balcony—crossed her arms and studied Kathy's cage.

"Well, go on," she said to the man. "Say what you needed to say. What you insisted on *only* saying in front of our captives."

While one valkyrie averted her eyes, the other one—the one with the softer expression—touched the man's arm.

"Thomas, if it is important, you need to say it."

"Eir, do not patronize him."

"I was not—"

"Just say what you need to say, warrior," the stern one demanded.

"Brynhildr…" the other valkyrie said as a warning. "Go easy. He is still new."

Samantha's head was spinning trying to follow the conversation. Worse, she was afraid that this extra attention would mean that she and Kathy wouldn't be able to devise a plan to get out of here.

"New or not, he is wasting our time," Brynhildr said. She turned back to Thomas. "Go on. Spit it out. We do not have all day."

The man cleared his throat and nodded in Kathy's direction. "I know her."

Brynhildr's eyes grew large as outrage took over her. Eir put her arm on his shoulder with her brow furrowed.

"What do you mean?" she asked.

Samantha waited for his answer and the valkyries' reaction to it, which could decide the fate of the witches' lives.

"I know her," he repeated.

"You." Brynhildr looked directly at Kathy's cage. "Explain yourself."

Samantha wished she could see her sister's face. Using her new power, she pushed into Kathy's mind and read her thoughts.

Deny it, she thought. *Admitting I was there would be confirming what they assume—that I started Ragnarök.* "Where do you know me from?" Kathy asked the man.

"From the alley," he said. "Where I died."

Samantha felt her heart drop into her stomach. What were the valkyries going to do to them now? Just as Kathy thought, he basically confirmed what the valkyries were assuming.

Brynhildr and Eir both turned to the other valkyrie.

"Herja," Brynhildr said, "you were there. Is he being truthful?"

Herja looked into Kathy's cage with fierce eyes. "Yes, she was there that night."

"I knew it!" Brynhildr cried out. "This is further proof that we are preparing for the final battle! Prepare the army! These two are the first to die!"

"Wait a minute!" Herja yelled.   "What is it?" Eir guided Thomas back behind her so the three valkyries were face-to-face with the witches.

"We only know Ragnarök is starting when Heimdall sounds his horn," Herja said. "We have not heard his alarm yet."

Suddenly, Samantha felt Brynhildr's eyes bore into her and she took a step back deeper into the cage.

"How did you get into Asgard?" The valkyrie stepped toward Samantha's cage with a menacing look. "How did you persuade Heimdall to allow you entry? The only ones he allows to come and go through the gates of Asgard are gods, valkyries, and the souls we collect. And yet you slipped through. How?"

Herja and Eir both looked at her expectantly too.

Gently, Eir asked, "We have not had the chance to speak about your intentions."

"Because my intentions are good!" Samantha blurted. "Heimdall understood that! That's why he let me in!"

"Are you a god?" Herja asked. "You are certainly not a valkyrie and I have doubt you are a spirit."

Samantha shook her head. "I'm a witch. I'm only here to save my sister and go home. Neither of us wanted any of this trouble. If you let us go, we'll go home and won't tell anyone—"

Brynhildr put up her fist to silence her. "I have heard enough. You are exactly where you belong."

Herja leaned in and lowered her voice, but in the vast empty space, Samantha could still hear. "What if they are telling the truth?"

"It would explain why Heimdall allowed her entry," Eir reasoned. "And we brought this other witch to Asgard ourselves."

Brynhildr shook her head. "I do not like it. We captured the first witch before she had a chance to blurt our secrets to everyone."

"She is a witch," Herja said. "She has her own secrets."

"Then how do you explain the second witch?" Brynhildr asked.

Eir looked at Samantha. "She said she only wanted to rescue her sister, which is a noble act."

"And how did she get by Heimdall?" Brynhildr asked.

Neither Herja nor Eir had a response to that. Both valkyries averted their eyes.

"I have a theory," Brynhildr said when the other two didn't come up with a response. "He has been at his post for centuries and has not acted as a god in quite some time. Therefore, he is more susceptible to witchcraft."

"I'm sorry that we got mixed up in all of this," Kathy said. "We didn't mean for any of this to happen. If you don't believe us, take us to Odin and we can explain—"

"Absolutely not!" Brynhildr blurted. She turned to the other valkyries. "Do you see? This was their plan! Infiltrate our borders and persuade us to deliver them directly to Odin so they can kill our leader."

"We're witches," Samantha said. "We don't have the power to kill a god."

"But you got past Heimdall," Brynhildr said.

"Is he dead?" Samantha asked.

Brynhildr was quiet.

"If he had perished at the hands of the enemy, there would be nothing stopping the enemy army from swarming Asgard and starting the war," Eir told Brynhildr.

"Odin is more powerful than Heimdall," Herja added. "He drinks from Mimir's well and has enough wisdom to determine if these witches are trustworthy. Much better than we can."

"He is due for an update anyway," Eir said. "Especially if we believe Ragnarök may be imminent."

Brynhildr grumbled. "All right. We will take the witches. But he goes back." She pointed to the man standing behind Eir.

"He needs to rest up. We cannot have even one man tired if we are about to march into battle."

Eir and Herja each stepped forward to unlock the cages.

"If you are tempted to use your powers, you will be severely punished," Eir warned when she freed Samantha.

"Same goes for you," Herja said to Kathy.

The sisters stepped out into the arena and caught a glimpse of one another. Brynhildr had started marching off toward the doorway out of the arena. Herja was beside Kathy leading her and Eir had a grip on Samantha's arm. Behind them, Thomas walked off back to his chambers.

As the witches were led out of Valhalla and onto the quiet night streets of Asgard, Samantha probed into Kathy's mind for a moment and confirmed that they were both thinking the same thing.

Hopefully Odin believes their story.

CHAPTER 26

All three valkyries grew grim the closer they got to Odin's hall. It was easily the largest building in Asgard, visible from nearly everywhere. A large sandstone structure with rounded corners and a large dome in the center.

The valkyries led the witches up the stone steps and through the main entrance. Inside, Samantha and Kathy both looked around at the ornately painted ceilings, the tall columns, and the marble floors.

It was dark inside, lit only by candlelight and several fireplaces. The sun had set, making the large windows that stretched from floor to ceiling essentially useless until daybreak.

Samantha and Kathy followed the valkyries through the main reception hall to a hallway off the side that passed by several other rooms as it meandered to an oak door near the back of the building at the end of the hall.

Brynhildr knocked three times and waited. She exchanged nervous glances with her other two compatriots and waited for the answer.

On the other side of the door, they could hear grumbling and muttering until it flung open. Wrapped in a long red robe stood a man with a graying beard and shoulders nearly as wide as the door. He was barefoot and looked harried, likely because he had been woken from a sound sleep.

"Ladies, what is it? Did Heimdall sound the alarm? Who are these two?"

"Do you have a minute to talk, sir?" Brynhildr asked. "We seem to have a…dilemma."

Odin readjusted his robe and opened the door wider, permitting them in. Pulling a torch from its mount on the wall, he stuck the end in the fire roaring in the fireplace to light it, then handed it off to Herja to light the rest of the torches in the room.

Unlike the intricate floors in the reception hall, the one in Odin's chamber was uneven stone, beautified only by several decorative rugs. There was a solid table to one side of the room and an ornate four-poster bed with ruffled sheets on the other side. Beside the door to the hall was another door leading someone else.

Eir and Brynhildr brought Samantha and Kathy to the table

and had them sit with their hands on the tabletop. When Herja finished bringing more light to the room, she took a seat between the sisters.

Odin closed the door and stood with his arms crossed, towering over them. Intimidating, even for someone in a robe with bedhead.

"Go on," he said. "Tell me what is so important that you needed to alert me in the middle of the night."

"Sir, I am afraid this may be my fault," Herja started, but Odin held up his hand.

"I am not interested in assigning blame. I only want to know what the problem is to plan for a solution."

She nodded. "I was in Midgard two nights ago to collect the soul of Thomas Wilson, a police officer from Erie who had made his final fall. Before I was able to do so, however, this woman—" She put her hand on the table in front of Kathy. "—saw me and called out to me."

"She *saw* you?" he asked.

"Yes, sir," Herja said quietly.

"All of our normal precautions were in place, sir," Brynhildr added.

Odin nodded and looked back to Herja to continue.

"I brought this information back to the rest of the valkyries and we took this as a sign that Ragnarök was about to begin."

"But you did not hear Heimdall's alarm?" he asked.

"No, sir," she said. "We thought that maybe I had stumbled

on a sign that would come *before* the enemy marched on Asgard."

"I see."

"We went right back to Midgard and collected her," Brynhildr said. "There, we learned she was a witch."

Odin's eyebrows raised. "A witch? Interesting."

"It is another reason why we believe her seeing Herja in Midgard is a sign that Ragnarök is beginning," Brynhildr explained.

"Has she been a threat to you since you began holding her captive?" he asked.

Brynhildr and Herja glanced at each other before Brynhildr responded, "No, sir."

"And has she attempted to use any of her witchcraft on you?"

"No, sir."

He waved his hand. "Then let them go. I do not believe they are a threat to us. Heimdall will announce the start of Ragnarök with the sound of his horn."

"Sir, the witch's sister was able to enter Asgard without Heimdall sounding the alarm," Brynhildr said.

Odin's eyes widened as he locked them on Samantha, who felt the intensity of his stare in her soul. "Did she now?"

"It was only because my intentions were pure," Samantha said quickly. "Heimdall understood that I only wanted to save—"

He put up his hand to silence her. "Enough. I will not be spoken to by prisoners."

Samantha gulped, but tried to focus her new power on probing Odin's mind. She didn't expect it to work because he was a god, but she had managed to view some of the thoughts in Heimdall's mind so it was worth a shot.

But it didn't work. As hard as she pushed, she heard nothing but silence. Saw nothing but his hard gaze as he studied her.

"Brynhildr, Herja, Eir. All three of you have failed me in your mission to serve me."

Herja began to rebut. "Sir, we did not want to alarm you—"

"You withheld information about intruders in Asgard from me," Odin said. "That was a dangerous decision that could have harmed the lives of everyone living here."

"That's why you should let us go!" Kathy said.

Odin's eyes flashed with anger and he pointed toward the door. "Valkyries, take them to the courtyard and execute them. They will not be threats to us any longer."

Eir gave Samantha a mournful look, but stood and hooked her hand under the witch's arm.

"No!" Samantha cried out. "You can't do this! We did nothing to hurt you!"

Eir and Herja both dragged the witches toward the door, which Brynhildr held open for them. The witches continued to shout and tried to squirm out of the valkyries' grip, but there was a strong hold on them.

"Herja, you saw me," Kathy said. "You know I didn't attack you first! You came after me! And even after you brought me here, I haven't done anything but try to escape!"

"I am sorry," Herja said. "But I am Odin's servant and I listen to his orders."

"Wait!" Kathy turned her attention to Odin, who stood watching the scuffle. She remembered something from her conversation with Herja before. "Ragnarök won't begin until Loki escapes, right? And they think me seeing Herja means that Loki has escaped and is planning an attack by weakening your defenses, right?"

Odin nodded, but offered nothing else.

"So there's an easy way to prove that we're innocent," Kathy said. "Go find Loki's cage. If he's still there, that means that when I saw Herja in Erie, it was just an accident and not a sign of the final battle. If he's not there…then I guess you have no choice but to execute us and prepare for war."

Samantha watched as Odin considered it with growing interest. She was afraid of the possibility that perhaps Loki *did* escape, completely unrelated to Kathy seeing Herja, and they'd be executed anyway. But at this point, this was their only hope.

"You present an interesting theory," Odin finally said. "Valkyries, new orders. Take the witches to check on Loki's chambers. Make sure he is still there. If he is not and you encounter trouble, use the witches as sacrifices to save yourself until you can deploy your army."

CHAPTER 27

Immediately after receiving their new orders, the valkyries led Samantha and Kathy out of Odin's hall, through the streets of Asgard, and back onto the Bifröst rainbow bridge where Heimdall protected the gate. The valkyries offered him a curt nod as they passed and he returned a confused look to Samantha, who did her best to avoid meeting his eyes.

Nobody talked as they marched down Bifröst, descending first into the clouds, then overlooking the snowy and rocky surface of the earth before stepping off the rainbow bridge onto a dirt trail on a mountainside. Pine trees rose up toward the sky in between moss-covered rocks. Across the valley, snow-topped mountains stretched out. It would've been beautiful if the circumstances were different.

VALKYRIE

By time their feet touched the earth again, both Samantha and Kathy were sore and tired and weak as a result of their small meals and lack of sleep. Worse, the air was cold. It seemed like Bifröst protected them from the elements, but as soon as they were one hundred percent back in Midgard, they felt the bitter chill of the high altitude. That included wind blowing through the mountains.

Neither women were dressed for the temperature, having picked out their clothes thinking they were going to spend a hot August day in Erie. Even the valkyries didn't appear to be dressed for it, but they didn't seem to mind and continued marching without even the slightest shiver.

"How much longer is it?" Kathy asked Herja, who marched beside the witch to make sure she was keeping pace.

"No talking," Brynhildr said firmly from the lead.

"But we're cold," Samantha said. "We didn't think we'd be hiking a mountain." Then again, they didn't think they'd spend the night in Valhalla either.

"Keep moving and you will stay warm." Brynhildr continued pressing on along the narrow, rocky path that zigzagged along the side of the mountain, climbing higher.

The witches stayed quiet as they followed. They both knew that there was no sense in arguing. Kathy tried to focus on plodding along. One foot in front of the other.

Distractions only went so far, though. After a while, both sisters were losing feeling in their fingers and their shivers became constant with each bitter gust of wind blowing through.

Finally, Brynhildr stopped and looked toward the base of a tree protruding up from the side of a hill on the mountain. If it hadn't been pointed out, Kathy would've missed it, but now that she saw it she could tell something sinister lied within.

Outside the cave, there was melted snow, dried-up and dying moss, and the tree that the cave mouth was hidden beneath had several branches with no needles.

"This is it," Brynhildr confirmed.

"Now what?" Samantha rubbed her hands up and down her arms.

"Now we enter," Eir said softly.

Kathy swung around and looked at her. "I'm not going in there."

"You go or you die," Brynhildr said. "Those were our orders."

"Do not be afraid," Eir assured Kathy as she ushered them in after Brynhildr. Herja brought up the rear.

Impossibly, the temperature dropped even colder once they entered the cave. Damp, smelly, and pure darkness. The only solace was that there was no wind. From somewhere deeper in the cave, water dripped and Kathy remembered watching something on the Discovery Channel about how water in a cave meant that the cave was unstable and more likely to collapse.

Yet that didn't scare Kathy nearly as much as what else she heard. The faint sound of a hissing snake. A new set of goosebumps grew all over her skin that had nothing to do with the temperature. Her heart pounded and every instinct in her told her to run. And yet she followed the valkyries deeper inside along with her sister.

As they rounded a corner, Brynhildr stopped short and a woman with wild, dry gray hair stood in front of them holding a bowl. She had a hooked nose and seemed to be missing a few teeth, but that didn't stop her from laughing hysterically.

"Ah! I see we have guests! To what do I owe the pleasure?"

CHAPTER 28

Kathy let out an involuntary yelp when she saw the woman appear. Samantha instinctively grabbed her sister's arm and pulled her back until she bumped into Eir, who stood behind them.

Herja took a step forward beside Brynhildr. "What do you want, Sigyn?"

"Sigyn?" Kathy asked.

"Loki's wife," Eir murmured from behind the witches.

Sigyn looked around Brynhildr and Herja to speak directly to Kathy. "I have been imprisoned here just like my husband."

"You have not!" Brynhildr said sternly. Her voice carried up and down the cave.

"I have too!" Sigyn argued. She looked back at Kathy. "Did

they tell you how my dear, loving husband's confinement consists of a large serpent continuously dripping its venom onto him? I bet they left that part out." She brought her eyes back to Brynhildr and looked her up and down. "Unlike those of you in Asgard, I have a heart and I will not sit by and watch my husband squirm as he is slowly killed."

"You are twisting his sentencing to appear as though you are the martyr," Herja said.

"I am not." Sigyn indicated the bowl she carried. "If I did not collect the venom and toss it out of the cave, Loki would have died long ago."

Samantha and Kathy exchanged looks. That explained the dead vegetation around the mouth of the cave. The whole place gave off a sense of death.

"Of course, that was very likely your plan," Sigyn added. "You wanted to get rid of us both so you trapped him in this hellhole, knowing I would follow! So yes, dear valkyrie, I may as well be imprisoned just like my husband is."

Brynhildr looked like she was about to erupt, but Samantha spoke up instead.

"Excuse me, I'm sorry. We don't want to disturb you or your husband."

"Then what are you doing here?" Sigyn snapped. "I no longer have time for chitchat. I need to return to my husband's side to make sure he will live to see another day. Each passing second brings him more pain and misery. Another part of my own sentence: watching my husband suffer each and every day. And now you are here to distract me!" She tried to push past the valkyries but stopped when neither Brynhildr nor Herja would budge.

"We're here for a reason," Samantha said. "Odin sent us to make sure that Loki is still locked up."

"Why would he not be?" Sigyn narrowed her eyes and studied Samantha. "Who are you? You are not a valkyrie—certainly not a god. And judging by the fact that you arrived with valkyries, I think it is safe to assume that you are not mere mortals, either."

"We're witches," Kathy said. "We just want to go check on Loki and then report back to Odin."

Sigyn hooked a thin eyebrow. "Witches?" She looked back at Brynhildr and Herja. "Not only do you come to jeer at your captive as he dies a slow death, but you bring an *audience* to add to his torment?"

"That is not what is happening," Brynhildr said. "Stand aside and let us pass. The longer you argue with us, the longer Loki will suffer without your assistance."

"Which is what *you* have wanted all along!" Sigyn spat.

Brynhildr took a step toward the woman, but Sigyn tossed the contents of the bowl toward Samantha and Kathy. So many things happened at once, all in an effort to save the witches.

Eir pulled Samantha and Kathy back, falling onto the rocky floor.

Herja jumped back and spread her arms and legs wide to try to cover the sisters.

Brynhildr lunged in front of the group, taking the full force of the collection of venom.

"Is everyone okay?" Samantha asked, meeting eyes with Kathy.

"Yeah." Kathy looked over and saw Brynhildr on the floor, convulsing.

"Brynhildr!" Eir cried out.

CHAPTER 29

Samantha and Kathy both scrambled over to Brynhildr to try to save her from whatever Sigyn threw at her. At the very least, they could help keep her head from slamming against the rocks as she seized.

Samantha's hands were only an inch away from Brynhildr's head when Eir cried out from behind her.

"Do not touch her!"

The sisters immediately pulled their hands away.

"The snake venom would do the same to you," Eir said.

Samantha and Kathy looked at each other and exchanged a look of fear. They both felt helpless as they sat beside Brynhildr, who only a moment ago stood so strong and was now perhaps the most vulnerable she'd ever been in her life—and the witches could do nothing to help her.

Sigyn laughed and flashed her rotten teeth. "Ding dong, the valkyrie is dead!"

Herja shot to her feet, jumped over Brynhildr's twitching body, and swung her spear around, smashing it against Sigyn's smiling face. Loki's wife crumpled to the floor and within seconds, Herja had the tip of her blade at the woman's throat.

"Stand down," Herja told her. "Or so help me, I will kill you and then there will be no one to save your husband from his torment."

Sigyn made choking sounds as Herja pressed the blade further against her exposed neck.

With her eyes still locked on the woman, Herja spoke to Eir, Samantha, and Kathy. "Go check on Loki. Make sure he is still there. We need to return to Asgard without anymore losses."

The remaining three looked down at Brynhildr's body, which had stopped twitching and now lay still with a deadly, icy stare at nothing in particular.

Samantha took a step forward but stopped as the ground began to shake again. "What's that?" she asked.

"I do not know," Eir said softly, looking down the cave.

"I can't imagine it's anything good," Kathy added.

The ground continued to quake, more violently with each passing second. Everyone fell to the ground as bits and pieces of rock, stone, and dirt fell from the ceiling of the cave.

"Loki!" Sigyn cried out, but kept her head low like the others.

Samantha and Kathy hunkered close to one another, covering their heads, hoping the shaking would stop. Neither of them had ever experienced an earthquake and this was the closest they came to it.

From deep inside the cave, something burst, like a tree snapping in a thunderstorm. What followed was a deep roar that echoed through the cave and brought an end to the violent shaking of the earth.

Slowly, Samantha and Kathy picked up their heads. They each brushed off the dirt and other debris that had fallen on them as they took inventory of everyone else.

"Is everyone okay?" Samantha asked again.

One by one, they each indicated in one way or another that they were unharmed, only shaken.

Herja quickly pointed her spear at Sigyn again. "*You* stay where you are."

Instead, Sigyn shot to her feet and ran deeper into the cave. "Loki!"

"*Sigyn!*" Herja bellowed. "I told you to *stop*!"

This time, she listened and turned to face the witches and the valkyries. "The earthquake was from Loki shaking from the serpent venom. If it stopped, it means that Loki is dead!"

Herja and Eir exchanged looks with one another while Samantha and Kathy did the same. At least that answered the question they came here for: Loki was still locked up like he was supposed to be and the witches hadn't started Ragnarök. Or, he *was* locked up. What would Odin say now that Loki was dead? And how much revenge would Sigyn seek? Would she be just as much a threat as Loki would've been?

Before the valkyries could give another order to Sigyn, she turned to continue deeper into the cave, only stopping when the ground shook again briefly.

"If Loki's dead, then what the hell was that?" Kathy asked.

Nobody answered her question, afraid of the possibilities.

Several seconds later, the ground shook briefly yet again. Then again.

Samantha narrowed her eyes. "It sounds like—"

"Footsteps," Eir finished.

Sigyn jumped in place and clapped her hands. "Loki! Loki! Is that you? Honey, I knew you could do it! I knew I was helping you build your strength all these years to finally kill that serpent!"

"Kill the serpent?" Herja asked, then looked down at Brynhildr. "But if you were not collecting the venom, how did he survive?"

"The bowl I used to collect the venom was not endless," Sigyn explained. "I had to leave him every so often to empty it. Each time I did, he died a little more. So we created a plan to conserve his energy while I collected the venom. He only used what he needed to survive those moments where he was directly hit by the serpent's poison."

"So he's *stronger* than when he was put in here?" Kathy asked.

Sigyn let out a throaty laugh as the footsteps grew closer. "Yes!"

Kathy looked to her older sister with fear in her eyes. So far, their experience with gods hadn't been a good one. Their magic was virtually useless against them. How were they going to face someone who the gods even needed to lock up because they couldn't defeat him?

CHAPTER 30

The thumping footsteps grew more thunderous, shaking the rocky floor beneath them with each step. Finally, a man in tattered clothing rounded the corner. His dark hair was straggly and long, standing on end in all directions, which matched the look of his beard. He was thin, the details of his ribcage seen down his torso. On his wrists and his ankles he dragged thick chains wrapped around him.

"Loki! Loki! Loki!" Sigyn cheered when she met her husband. "It worked! You are free!"

Loki let out a hearty laugh with his wife and looked to the valkyries and the witches. "Thank you for freeing me!"

"No!" Herja said. "You are *not* free! Odin will—"

"Odin will not hear about this until it is too late." He looked down at Brynhildr's stiff body. "You four will suffer a similar fate."

Eir reached for Samantha and Kathy's arms, pulling them back toward the mouth of the cave. "Go," she told them. "Herja and I will keep him at bay."

"But we can help." Samantha eyed up Loki, who was able to stand fully upright in the cave, but only just. He towered over them, intimidating them.

"No," Eir said. "He is part god. Your powers will not work against him."

Kathy put up her hands and tried to freeze Loki. For a moment, it worked. He stood frozen in time.

"What is this?" Sigyn called out, staring at Kathy. "Witchcraft should not have any effect on him!"

As if on cue, Loki began to slowly move, first his arms, then his legs, then all at once he broke through Kathy's magic. Just as the valkyries had done back in Erie.

Instead of getting angry, Loki clutched his belly and laughed. "Wow! We are going to have some fun! Are you all ready?"

"Go," Eir said again, more panicked this time. She pushed at Samantha and Kathy, trying to get them to leave the cave, but both women stared transfixed at Loki.

Something was happening. He was changing. First, he began to fall forward face-down toward the rocky floor. But before he made contact, his body changed. Slowly, his skin grew as black as midnight, his arms melded into his side, and his legs morphed together. His face elongated and his teeth grew sharper, parting to allow his thin, forked tongue to slither through.

In a matter of seconds, Loki had changed from a large man to a large serpent.

"Oh no." Kathy reached for Samantha. "No, no, no. I don't do snakes!"

"After years of being tortured by a snake myself," Loki said with a slithering lisp, "I would love to see how the pure and mighty valkyries face against one!"

"Get out of here!" Eir bellowed at the sisters as she brandished her weapon and stepped beside Herja in preparation to fight.

Samantha and Kathy both looked back at Loki's new form. He stared at them with hunger in his eyes.

"What is the matter, girls? I will not *bite*!" He cackled before lunging at Eir and Herja, who both parried his attacks.

"Let's go," Kathy said. "They're trained for this battle. They're stronger than we are. They can handle this."

Finally, they both peeled their eyes away from the scene playing out before them and took off in a run back to the cave entrance.

CHAPTER 31

The brisk air outside of the cave that had tormented the sisters before was a breath of fresh air after they escaped the horrors that lived inside.

"What the hell do we do now?" Kathy took several steps away from the opening, wanting to put as much distance between them as possible.

Samantha looked back at the mouth of the cave, then out to the valley between the mountains, where there was no sign of anyone. "I think that we should find the Bifröst bridge, go back to Asgard, and have Heimdall sound the alarm. That will send the army the valkyries have been putting together to fight off Loki."

Kathy shook her head. "That would take too long. Do you

know how long it took us to get here from Asgard? And then to wait for the army to assemble and march here? Herja and Eir need help *now*."

"I know." Samantha stared at the mouth of the cave and rubbed her numb hands together.

"And that's assuming we can even see Bifröst," Kathy continued. "It's supposed to be invisible to us."

"So what do you suggest we do?" Samantha snapped. "We're fresh out of options and I know neither of us would feel comfortable just leaving them in there without at least *trying* to help them. It's not in our nature as witches."

"That might be our only option!"

"Why'd you have to go out to the club with Trisha?" Samantha snapped again. "On a Thursday night!"

"All right, ease up, Grandma," Kathy said as she rubbed her bare arms to stay warm. "Getting mad at each other is not going to help them. Especially if Herja and Eir are killed and Loki comes after us next. He's not going to want to risk word getting out to Odin. Loki's first step is to get out of that cave."

The sounds of slithering, the valkyries' grunts, and Sigyn's maniacal laugh blended together and carried from deep inside the cave.

"You just gave me an idea," Samantha said.

"I did?"

"We're witches."

"Yes, I'm aware of that," Kathy said. "But they're *gods*! Or, god-adjacent or whatever."

"No, I mean we can cast a spell to contain Loki—and Sigyn too, for that matter."

"Again, they're *gods*," Kathy said. "Our magic doesn't work on them. Or didn't you see how he unfroze himself?"

"We're not casting a spell on Loki himself, but on the cave that contains him," Samantha said. "We can come up with something that will keep him locked up even longer. I'm sure this is not the Ragnarök that the valkyries foresaw."

"Okay, but how do we keep Loki and Sigyn in there without trapping Herja and Eir too?" Kathy asked. "If we cast a spell on the cave, that would lock them in there too. They'd be as good as dead. This whole mess already cost Brynhildr her life. And that's even *if* the spell works."

"You need to believe it'll work, Kathy." Samantha started back to the cave.

Kathy took two steps toward her, but her fear kept her rooted where she was. "Where are you going?"

"Back into the cave," Samantha said. "You just start coming up with the spell. I'm going to get Herja and Eir out of there!"

"Sam!" Kathy called, but her sister had disappeared into the darkness of the cave. Kathy hugged herself and rubbed her arms to keep warm, trying not to think about how helpless she felt.

CHAPTER 32

Samantha ran into the cave at full force, but stopped short when she saw that Loki had pushed back Eir and Herja much closer to the mouth of the cave. The valkyries wielded their weapons, dodging strikes from Loki's large fangs. He was swift, evading most of their attempts to strike him and gain back some ground.

Beside her husband, Sigyn stood with a wide smile that showed off her rotten teeth and stretched her wrinkled face into what Samantha thought looked like a Halloween mask. Every so often, she offered her husband encouraging words:

"That is it, dear!"

"You almost have them!"

"Not much further until we are free!"

Samantha knew she needed to act fast. The valkyries looked like they were getting tired. They likely couldn't hold Loki back anymore.

"We have a plan!" she called out.

Eir chanced a quick look over her shoulder just before she dropped to her knee to duck under Loki's head, which he used to try to throw her into the cave wall.

"What are you doing in here?" Eir jabbed her spear in Loki's direction, but he recoiled and aimed his next attack at Herja.

"Get back outside!" Herja jumped off the cave wall and lunged toward the top of Loki's serpent head as he hissed at Eir. He turned quickly and opened his mouth. Eir stabbed her spear at his forked tongue and he snapped his mouth shut, just as Herja bounced off of him and landed flat on her back. She shot to her feet moments before Loki struck again.

"Get as far away from here as possible!" Eir told Samantha.

"Not without you two," the witch said defiantly.

"We're a little busy here." Herja's chest heaved, as did Eir's. They both had sweat glistening on them, despite the cold. Even in the short time that Samantha was watching, she noticed their jumps weren't as high, their attacks had less force, and their reflexes were sluggish. They were growing tired from the relentless attacks.

"It will not be long now!" Sigyn called out to Loki. "Finish them!"

Samantha took a cautious step forward and nearly got hit

with the end of Herja's spear as she swung it in another attack toward Loki. But Samantha was focused on Sigyn. More specifically, her mind.

Sure, Loki was too powerful to push influencing thoughts to, but what about Sigyn? Even if she was a god, she had spent the last several centuries running up and down this cave trying to save her husband from being poisoned. It obviously weakened her mind. Maybe it did the same to her powers that protected her mind.

Samantha had been able to mold Heimdall's mind with her new power. His had been weakened from standing guard outside the gates of Asgard for so long. She hoped Sigyn's mind was in the same—or worse—state.

Taking several careful steps backward in case the fight moved while she was in Sigyn's mind, Samantha locked eyes with Loki's wife and pushed her new power in her direction.

For several seconds nothing happened, but Samantha maintained her focus. Slowly, she began to see images, scenes, memories. Faint, at first, but they grew more defined and they all seemed to pass by her quickly.

Loki and Sigyn's life in Asgard. Sigyn's life was quiet, but she lived in constant fear that her husband's antics would get him in trouble.

The prophesied death of Odin's son, Balder, who everyone loved. Loki came home laughing that he had carved a spear out of mistletoe and given it to Balder's brother, Hoder, who was blind, and persuaded him to throw it at Balder. The mistletoe spear pierced Balder's heart and killed the beloved god.

Hel, the Queen of the Dead, allowing Balder to come back to life. Her only stipulation was that everyone in Asgard needed to mourn for him. Loki, however, refused to weep, despite Sigyn's attempts to get him to.

Hel refusing the let Balder come back to life. Odin soon found out that Loki was the reason and sentenced him to banishment to pay for their loss. Loki's containment in the cave. His and Sigyn's own son, Narfi, provided the chains that shackled Loki beneath the poisonous serpent. Sigyn devoted her life to collecting the dripping venom in a bowl in an attempt to keep her husband alive.

Sigyn's many trips to the mouth of the cave to dispose of the venom. Each time she left, the earth shook violently as Loki seized from the impact of the serpent's venom.

As the memories came to Samantha, she felt for Sigyn. Saw how she was only trying to be a loyal wife, to protect her husband. But through those memories, it was evident to Samantha that Loki could never be free. He couldn't be trusted and he could hardly be contained. She only hoped the spell Kathy came up with would work.

There was another thing Samantha gained from viewing Sigyn's memories: it was very apparent that Sigyn was loyal to her husband. She was the only one who stood by his side through the length of his imprisonment. At the root of their relationship, no matter how twisted they were, was love. Loki would want to save her just as much as she wanted to save him all these years trapped in the cave.

Once Samantha was deep in Sigyn's mind, she pushed influence in her direction as well. Slowly, the witch took control of Sigyn's body through her mind. Just the twitch of a finger at first, then her whole hand, and finally her legs.

It took so much of Samantha's energy to get Sigyn to move, but it worked. Slowly, Sigyn took several steps in front of Loki, turned, and stared up at her husband.

Immediately, Loki pulled back and stared at his wife.

"What?" he asked in his slithery tongue. "What is it?"

Herja and Eir stood back and breathed heavy, grateful for the break in fighting.

"Sigyn, what is the matter?" Loki's long snake form changed, returning to his rightful appearance of a large man with the crazed hair.

Quickly, Samantha pulled out of Sigyn's mind and reached for the valkyries. Her vision momentarily went dark from the disorientation and she was lightheaded—the fact that she hadn't eaten in quite some time didn't help—but Herja and Eir both took the hint and helped Samantha run out of the cave.

Their escape, however, didn't go unnoticed.

"Hey!" Loki called after them. "Get back here! We are not finished!"

CHAPTER 33

As Samantha, Herja, and Eir ran out of the mouth of the cave, they heard the roar from Loki behind them.

"There you guys are!" Kathy said. "He sounds pissed."

"He is," Samantha said. She stood beside her sister and leaned on her because her head was still spinning from being inside of Sigyn's mind. The new power would take some getting used to. "Do you have the spell?"

"I came up with something," she said. "I hope it's enough."

"He is coming!" Herja waved her spear at the mouth of the cave.

"Your magic will not work on him!" Eir said.

"We found a workaround," Kathy said.

The ground vibrated as Loki's pounding footsteps emanated

from inside the cave. His roar closely followed, drawing nearer the more he ran.

"All right, let's go," Samantha said. "Sigyn being disoriented bought us a few minutes for her to pull herself together, but he's on the move so let's get this show on the road."

"Repeat after me," Kathy said.

Samantha nodded and together they recited:

Loki, Loki, foolish deity,
As your punishment, you can't be free.
Although you have escaped your capture,
We seal this cave until the rapture.

Loki approached the mouth of the cave just as the sisters' magic took effect. A sheer light shone over the mouth of the cave and moments later, Loki bounced off of the invisible wall and fell backward, sending more vibrations across the mountain that rattled the needles in the pine trees around them.

Beside him, Sigyn appeared. She rubbed her forehead, but stopped short when she seemed to hit the forcefield as well.

"Looks like it worked!" Kathy cheered. She raised her fists in the air, but quickly brought her arms down and shivered.

Samantha smiled. "Good job with the spell."

Herja and Eir watched as Loki and Sigyn knocked on the invisible force trapping them.

"Will that contain them?" Eir asked.

Samantha nodded. "It should."

"Odin may want to send in reinforcements and restrain Loki in the way that he was," Kathy added. "Maybe even add another snake, as much as I hate them. It seemed to work, though."

Herja nodded. "We will see to it that Loki cannot escape. At least not until the time is right."

"We are sorry to cause you two so much trouble," Eir added. "It appears as if you were telling the truth all along."

Kathy nodded.

"We're sorry that it had to come with the loss of Brynhildr," Samantha said. "I wish we could at least bring her body back to Asgard for a proper burial."

"Thank you for your condolences," Eir said, "but Brynhildr's body—and spirit—will be with the earth now, where she belongs."

"She is at peace," Herja added.

"I'm sure she is," Samantha said.

"If we're all set here, can we get back someplace warm?" Kathy asked, shivering. "My toes are most certainly *not* at peace."

Eir smiled. "Herja will escort you back. I will stay here and stand guard until Loki has been more properly contained."

"Do you think we'll be free to go home?" Samantha asked.

Herja started to lead them back toward where they exited Bifröst. "That will be for Odin to decide."

CHAPTER 34

In the daylight, Odin looked much more like the war god that he was than he did the previous evening when the valkyries woke him. He stood in the center of the entry room in his hall with his arms crossed. He wore a red tunic around him and a fur cloak over his shoulders that made him look even bigger than his brute size.

Herja led Samantha and Kathy toward him. The witches both looked around at all the eyes staring at them, watching them enter. The hall was packed, but eerily quiet. There were others dressed in tunics and laced boots standing around the hall with carts and tables containing produce, meats, items of clothing, and more.

"We have returned with news, sir." Herja bowed her head

briefly once she stood in front of Odin. She looked up and met his eyes.

"You are missing two of your own," he said.

"Yes, unfortunately, Brynhildr has perished at the hands of Loki's wife Sigyn."

Odin hooked an eyebrow and cast glances at both Samantha and Kathy. "Loki's wife?"

"Yes, sir," Herja said. "When we arrived, Sigyn was on her way out of the cave to deposit the venom she collected from the serpent in Loki's containment. She and Brynhildr exchanged words."

"What kind of words?" Odin asked.

"Sigyn felt as though she were a captive like her husband."

"Nonsense. Nothing is keeping her there except her love for her husband, whatever she may see in him."

"And that is more or less what Brynhildr told her," Herja said. "Before we could get down to the end of the cave to check on Loki's confinement, an earthquake erupted."

"An earthquake?"

"Yes, sir. According to Sigyn, it was from Loki shaking so bad from the snake venom. And then it stopped."

"Has he finally perished?"

Herja shook her head. "No, sir. He defeated the serpent. He walked out to us, changed into a snake himself—"

"How fitting," Odin added.

"At that point, Sigyn had already taken the opportunity to

throw the venom she held in her bowl at Brynhildr and…she did not make it."

The god of war bowed his head and the room was quiet as many others did the same. Samantha and Kathy followed suit out of respect.

"So where is Eir?" Odin asked. "Has she passed on as well?"

"No, sir. When Loki turned into a snake, he began attacking us. It was all Eir and I could do to keep him in the cave. We barely escaped."

"And where were these two during all of this?" Odin asked. He looked at the witches. "I thought you were supposed to protect people from harm?"

"We—" Samantha started, but Herja held out her hand to stop her.

"They did," the valkyrie said. "We told them to leave, but they came back. To save us. These witches used their powers to keep Loki contained so that we could escape. And then they sealed the cave with their magic."

"Sealed the cave?" Odin asked. "What are you talking about?"

"We put a magical barrier on it," Samantha explained.

"You may want to add another serpent or something to Loki's cave," Kathy added. "Witch magic and god powers are kind of on two different levels, if you know what I mean."

Odin studied them, but did not offer anything else.

"These witches deserve to return to their regular lives as a thank you for helping us maintain Loki's capture," Herja explained. "It was…it was a mistake to bring them here in the first place."

Again, Odin's face looked impassive. Hard to read. He stared at the witches, looking between both Samantha and Kathy as he considered what Herja had said. All around them, the others in the hall watched on in quiet wonder as well.

Finally, Odin uncrossed his arms and set his hands on his hips. "You witches have given us quite the runaround, have you not?"

Not sure what to say, the sisters remained silent.

"I suppose you have proven that you mean us no harm," he continued. "You may go home."

Smiles broke out on both witches' faces.

"On one condition," he added. "You must keep the secret of the valkyries and Asgard to yourself. There will be no talk to anyone, especially believers of Norse mythology, about all that you have witnessed these past few days. Do you understand?"

"Yes!" Samantha said quickly. "Yes, we just want to go home."

"As you wish," he said with a grin. He looked back to the valkyrie. "Herja, will you please escort these ladies back to where they came from?"

Kathy held up her hand. "Excuse me, I just have one quick request."

"What are you doing?" Samantha murmured.

Ignoring her, Kathy continued, "Would it be terribly inconvenient if I spoke to Tommy real quick before we go? It's just, this all started when I watched him die. I don't want to just leave him."

Odin turned to Herja. "That would be up to the valkyries, since he is a part of their army. As long as the exchange is brief, I do not see the harm."

Herja looked over at Kathy and nodded. "I suppose that could be allowed."

"Thank you!" Kathy said.

"Herja," Odin said. "I trust that you will make sure these women are taken care of? Ladies, I wish you well on your journey."

CHAPTER 35

The one thing that was difficult to adjust to in Asgard was that wherever the sisters went, eyes followed them. Stepping back into Valhalla was no different. Every one of the members of the army noticed their return. Some resumed fighting shortly after they entered, but many watched as Herja led the witches through the crowd to where Tommy and several other men and women in police uniforms stood. " T h o m a s Wilson," Herja said. "You have visitors."

Tommy looked up, the surprise of seeing Kathy again evident on his face.

"You're back," he said.

Kathy smiled. "Yeah."

"Would you two like to go somewhere more private?" Herja asked.

"This will just take a second," Kathy assured her.

Samantha and Herja both stood to the side. Herja looked around at the rest of the army staring. Before she could say anything, several other valkyries from around the arena called out to the army to tell them to resume their training.

When the noise level of the room increased again and Kathy and Tommy were no longer the center of attention, she took a step toward him so he could hear her better.

"I just wanted to apologize for not being able to save you the other day," Kathy said.

Tommy shrugged and looked down.

"I'm sure you've caught on by now, but I'm much more than your average person," she said with a chuckle. "I'm a witch. And one of my responsibilities as a witch is to protect people. I wasn't able to protect you that night and I'm sorry."

"It wasn't your fault," he said. "You walked out right at the end. And, from what I've heard, apparently that's what was supposed to happen. I don't know. I never really believed in that kind of stuff before, but it's hard to argue with all of this."

"I'm sure it's a lot to process," she said. "I don't envy you."

He laughed likely. "Gee, thanks."

"You know what I meant."

"I'm adjusting," he said while nodding. "It's hard to wrap my head around the fact that my life is over, but I know now that my mission isn't finished yet. I have a bigger purpose here. I'm going to bring about a new, more beautiful world."

"That's good. I'm glad you're looking at it that way," Kathy said. "I wouldn't want you just moping around."

"Yeah." Tommy slipped his hands in his pockets and then met her eyes. "Do you mind if I ask a favor of you? I'd do it, but I have training to complete for the foreseeable future."

Kathy smiled again. "Sure, what is it?"

"Can you check on my wife? See how she's doing with…me being gone? And my daughter. She's just a baby, but she'll miss me soon enough."

Kathy's heart ached as she thought about his family back in Erie. "Tommy, I don't know—"

"It's just that I want them to know that I'm okay," he cut her off. "This wasn't my first choice, obviously, but I'm coming around to being okay with this. I want them to eventually be okay with it too."

She cleared her throat and looked down at their feet in the sandy floor, thinking of Odin's warning. "I'm not sure if I'll be able to tell them all of *that*, but I'll do my best to watch over them."

"Thanks."

"Besides, I'm sure they'll be fine," she went on. "They had a great role model to look up to. Someone I know they'll be turning to for comfort for the rest of their lives."

"I hope so," he said.

"Take care of yourself, Tommy," she said. "I hope you do well and I'll check on your family."

"Thank you," he said. "You have no idea how much that means to me. I'm going to do my best to make them proud."

"I'm sure they already are."

CHAPTER 36

I am so glad to be home," Samantha exclaimed as she and Kathy stepped through the front door of their house. She was exhausted and hungry and in need of a long shower. Most of all, she was dreading going back to work without really having a weekend off.

Samantha took a few steps into the house but something made her stop short. "Why are all the lights on?"

"You didn't leave them before you cast the spell to bring you to Asgard, did you?" Kathy asked.

"No—"

"Samantha?" Steven called from in the kitchen. He ran through the house and crashed into her, wrapping her tight in his arms. "I was so worried about you!" He pulled away to kiss her. "And Kathy! You're okay!" He reached over and gave her an awkward side hug.

"Steven, we're fine," Kathy said.

"You just disappeared on me," Steven said, addressing Samantha. "You were talking about the valkyries and Asgard and that Kathy was missing and then *you* went missing and—"

"I'm sorry." Samantha didn't realize that she had fallen off the face of the earth—quite literally—and what that would do to Steven. She thought of Tommy, being taken from his family so young and she cursed herself for having done that to Steven. If they had any kind of future together, she couldn't do anything like this again.

"I came back to talk to you yesterday, but you were gone," he said. "I called around to everyone I could think of and nobody had seen you. I was afraid you were..." Instead of finishing the sentence, he pulled her in for another hug.

"If it helps any, we did kind of save the world," Kathy added with a smirk.

"Kathy, do you mind?" Samantha raised her eyebrows, telling her sister, *Leave us alone.*

"Oh! Right! I will take advantage of your reunion and call dibs on the shower." She ran up the staircase and out of sight.

"I had no idea where you were or what was happening to you," Steven said. "I was so worried. I thought you might be—"

"But I'm not," Samantha said before he could say what they were both thinking. "Steven, I'm sorry for disappearing. And

I'm sorry you were worried, but now that you know I'm a witch, you have to understand that this is my life—although this *was* a little weirder than usual."

He nodded and looked down at their joined hands. "I know."

"As much as I'd love for you to be a part of my life, I know that this is a lot to take in," she went on. "So you need to decide, are you willing to put up with the parts of my life that are…inconvenient?" She rolled her eyes with a smile. "Dangerous, I mean. Let's not sugarcoat this. Being a witch is who I am. It's a packaged deal."

"Samantha, one thing I realized while you were gone is that I don't want to live without you," he said, meeting her eyes. "I love you for being you, and if being a witch is a part of who you are, I accept that. It's going to take some time for me to come around to it completely—to really wrap my head around it—but I want to do it at your side." He shrugged and smirked. "We both knew we'd keep learning new things about each other, right?"

"This is a big thing, though," she said.

"I know. And I'm okay with that. That's why, if you're still up for it, I'd like to keep planning the wedding. I want to be your husband."

Samantha sighed and pulled her hands away from his. She crossed her arms and took a step back to lean on the doorframe to the living room. "I'm not sure you realize everything you're signing on for if we get married. That's why I wanted to tell you

I was a witch before we got married, so you didn't feel like I pulled the wool over your eyes."

"Whatever it is, I can handle it."

"It seems like at least once a month we're chasing down some magical bad guy who is trying to hurt someone," Samantha went on. "And it always comes up at the most inconvenient times. That means plans will continue to be ruined when my witch duties call. That means our home becomes a potentially dangerous place from time-to-time. I mean, we're like the magical police!"

Steven smiled. "A lot of cops are married and have families."

"*And* this is something that Kathy and I will always need to do together. We're stronger together than we are apart."

"She's your sister, of course she's going to be in your life— *our* life."

Samantha shook her head and closed her eyes. "Steven, I'm just not sure you're really listening."

"I am. And I hear you. And I know there is plenty more that I don't know yet, but I don't care about any of that. I just want to be with you, which includes everything you're bringing to the table." He unfolded her arms and held her hands. "So what if our plans are ruined once in a while? I'm used to dealing with that already, at least now I'll have a better understanding as to why they're canceled."

"But this could be dangerous," Samantha pushed.

"And you've survived it all," Steven said. "I trust you. I trust your powers. I trust your intuition to do the right thing to protect yourself and the people you love."

Samantha stared at him. Saw how much he was pleading with her, the desperation evident in his eyes. He was just a man who was fighting to be with the woman he loved. But it was so much more complicated than that. As much as she told him about the magical interruptions and the deadly situations she found herself in again and again, until he lived it, he would never truly understand.

But the look in his eyes that seemed to fade the longer it took her to say something told her that she couldn't burst his bubble. This acceptance was what she wanted from him when she told him she was a witch. Now here he was, claiming to accept her for everything she was. She needed to give him a chance to really live this life with her as a witch.

Besides, the wedding wasn't until January. There was still time to postpone the wedding if he started having second thoughts.

"I just want to make sure you know everything you're getting into," Samantha said finally. "It's a lot more than the usual baggage. But I'd love to be able to call myself your wife."

He smiled wide and leaned forward to give her a kiss. When they parted, her squeezed her tight.

"Wait a minute," she said suddenly.

Steven pulled away and looked at her, confused. "What is it? What's wrong?"

"I haven't been reading your thoughts."

"Oh. That's right. I forgot you could do that. Did you lose that…ability?"

Samantha shook her head. "No, I had to use it to help save the valkyries from Loki, so I must've gotten enough of a hang on this new power to not invade people's minds."

Steven's eyes widened. "Loki? You actually saw him?"

She smiled. "I told you it was a lot."

"I guess so. But let's back up here. You're saying that you can't read minds anymore?"

She shook her head. "No, I can. But it's more of a conscious effort than passively collecting everyone's inner monologue."

"Oh," he said slowly, still confused.

"I promise you, I won't read your mind unless it's absolutely necessary," she said with a smirk. "There needs to be *some* mystery in a relationship. But don't think you can keep secrets from me!"

He laughed. "I wouldn't dare with a witch."

"And don't you forget it!"

CHAPTER 37

Hi, Milo? It's Kathy Walker. We met at the 814 on Thursday?" She was hunched over the kitchen counter with the phone pressed to her ear and her finger nervously coiling around the cord.

"Oh, hi," he said. It was different to hear his voice when he wasn't shouting over thumping music. "How are you?"

"I'm good." She smiled to herself. "Listen, I was thinking…um, I'm kind of at a crossroads in my life, of sorts. A lot of things are changing and I'm trying new things. Which I guess you don't need to know all those details." She laughed nervously.

"New things aren't a bad thing," he said with a similar chuckle.

"Yeah. And I've never really done this before—asked a guy out, especially one I met at a club—but do you think you'd want to grab coffee or something sometime? Somewhere where we *don't* have to shout at each other."

Milo laughed. "Yeah, I think that'd be great."

"Cool." She made a fist and brought it slowly to her forehead, cringing. This conversation was deeply awkward, but any new change would be awkward.

"Cool," he repeated. "Look, I'm kind of in the middle of work right now. But if you want to give me your number, I'll call you this afternoon and we can set something up."

"Sure." She smiled and gave him her number. When she hung up, she let out a loud groan, feeling completely exposed for pulling herself out of her comfort zone.

Kathy never usually had any trouble getting a date, but she was always the one being asked out. Never once had she ever asked anyone out. This was different for her, but she decided that if she was going to make an honest effort to move on from Jeremy, she needed to make changes in her life. She wasn't happy with the way things were going and that needed to change.

She picked up the newspaper from the table and flipped to the police blotter. There was an article about the arrest of Eugene "Dickie" Richards for the murder of Officer Thomas Wilson on Thursday night. It went along with several other previous charges, which included sexual assault. At least there was some level of justice being served for the loss of the Wilson family.

Grabbing Samantha's keys from the hook, Kathy stepped out the front door and locked it behind her. Samantha had gotten a ride into work from Steven, which gave Kathy free access of her car. Kathy had said she was going to go out and find a new job today—and it was certainly on her list—but she had other errands to run first.

Before she called Milo, Kathy had also called the police station and asked for the address of Officer Wilson so she could send his family a sympathy card. It took some convincing—the lady on the phone insisted Kathy send the card to the station instead—but Kathy finally got their address. It was the one thing that Tommy had failed to mention in Valhalla.

Within five minutes, Kathy was pulling onto Skyline Drive. She parked the car at the curb across the street from a modest blue ranch house. The garage door was closed and the small windows didn't offer her much insight into whether Tommy Wilson's wife and daughter were inside.

Wind blew through the open windows, providing relief from the muggy air. It was still hot, despite the cloudy sky. But Kathy wasn't about to complain about the heat after freezing her butt off over the weekend on her journey to Loki's cave.

Finally, after ten minutes, Kathy noticed the front door of the blue ranch open. A young woman with her blonde hair pulled back and large sunglasses covering her eyes stepped out with a stroller. Despite the rather ordinary task, Kathy could tell that the woman was suffering through her movements by the blank expression on her face. As if she were just going through the motions and felt completely numb.

Kathy stepped out of the car and approached her as she pushed the stroller toward the end of the driveway.

"Mrs. Wilson?"

Tommy's wife looked up and forced a smile. "I'm sorry, do I know you?"

Kathy shook her head. "No, but I knew your husband—briefly. I know what happened to him and I'm so, so sorry for your loss."

The fake smile faded and she sucked in her top lip as she nodded. "Thanks."

"I knew him from the club he worked at," Kathy went on. "He was always so nice to me. And I saw him protect a couple girls from some guys who didn't have good things on their minds."

"Yeah, he was a good man." Mrs. Wilson began pushing the stroller around Kathy and toward the street for a walk. "I'm sorry, but I really need to get going."

"Is this your daughter?" Kathy leaned into the stroller and wriggled her fingers on the little girl's belly. Her big eyes looked up at Kathy and her tiny fists waved in front of her. "She's cute."

"Thanks. She's about nine weeks old."

Kathy felt a pang of hurt in her heart for the woman. "I don't want to keep you or anything, I just wanted to offer my condolences and say that even though I didn't know Tommy *well*, I could tell he was a good person with a big heart who cared a lot about his family."   Mrs. Wilson's mouth turned down into a frown and she reached under her sunglasses to wipe her eyes. "He really was," she croaked.

Kathy touched the woman's arm to comfort her. She wanted to say more—wanted to say what Tommy had asked her to tell his wife—but couldn't think of how to do it without giving away that she knew more than she did.

"I just can't believe that he's gone," Mrs. Wilson went on. "I mean, I went to bed a wife and woke up a widow. He was only going to work!"

"I know. I can't imagine what you're going through. But I do know that Tommy's in a good place now."

Mrs. Wilson nodded. "In God's hands, right?"

Kathy smirked. "Something like that. You'll get to a good place too, but it sucks in the meantime."

Mrs. Wilson choked out a laugh between her tears. "Yes, it certainly does suck."

"Just remember that you'll always have a piece of your husband in your daughter." Kathy turned back to the baby who looked up at the tree branches above her swaying in the wind. "She's counting on you to be strong and to tell her how great her dad was."

"He'll be a part of her life," Mrs. Wilson said with a gentle nod. "Definitely."

"Anyway," Kathy said. "I didn't mean to make you cry or anything. I just wanted to tell you that I'm sorry for your loss and that I'm thinking about you."

Mrs. Wilson reached for Kathy's hand and squeezed it as she gave her a sad smile. "Thank you. I appreciate it."

"Good luck." Kathy returned to Samantha's car and started up the engine. She gave Mrs. Wilson a wave as she pulled away from the curb and drove out to the main route.

Instead of heading home, though, Kathy turned left onto W 38th Street off of Allegheny Road. She traveled over I-79, through the stoplights, and turned into Porreco College.

She had just told Mrs. Wilson that she and her daughter would find a good place eventually, but now it was Kathy's turn to find a good place. The way she was living her life now wasn't working as a long-term plan. She needed to be more responsible. More like her sister. If she was, they never would've gotten tangled up with the valkyries at all.

This was the first step to getting to a good place.

Samantha and Kathy's personal lives have been keeping them busy. Samantha's been planning her wedding, despite the frustrations of Steven's mother and the ensuing tension it creates between the bride and groom. Kathy is struggling with the coursework of her first college classes and spending enough time with Milo, the guy she's been dating.

Meanwhile, their new neighbors have invited them to a Halloween party. But the days leading up to the party reveal oddities and unusual behavior from the people in their lives, culminating in the witches' discovery at the party that a shapeshifter's been lurking among them all week.

With no idea who to trust, Samantha and Kathy have only a few hours to find out who the shapeshifter is and how to stop them before they can hurt anyone else—and the party just happens to be full of potential victims.

Shapeshifter is the fourth book in the Coven series, which serves as a prequel series to the Under the Moon series.

SHAPESHIFTER

COVEN: BOOK 4

Read on for an excerpt of the next book in
the Coven series!

DAVID NETH

CHAPTER 1

- OCTOBER 1988 -

Ruby Harding finished washing her face in the bathroom sink and reached for the towel on the rack beside her. She patted her face dry, looked in the mirror for any blemishes that needed attention, then turned off the bathroom light as she stepped into the hall.

At the top of the stairs, she stopped and listened for the sounds of movement below. Instead, she heard the TV and her husband's snores. He had fallen asleep on the couch *again*. They hadn't been married that long to be in a rut already, but here they were.

Ruby rolled her eyes and padded into the bedroom, where she had already turned on both bedside lamps and drawn the curtains. Pulling the blanket back, she crawled into bed.

SHAPESHIFTER

She was reading Stephen King's *Misery*. She'd slowly been working her way through his entire catalog for a few years now. The stories sometimes scared her so bad she had trouble sleeping. She figured she should probably stop reading these types of books before bed, but she couldn't help it. Horror books made her feel alive, which was more than could be said about her relationship with her husband as of late.

Ruby opened the book and got started on the next chapter. She was three pages in when she heard the floorboards creak from downstairs.

Finally, Eli is coming to bed, she thought. When she glanced at the clock, she couldn't help but feel a little disappointed. He usually stayed down there for another half hour, which gave her ample peace and quiet time by herself to read.

Okay, so maybe she didn't totally hate the fact that he fell asleep on the couch.

Turning back to her book, she read another half page before she heard the distinct murmur of voices from downstairs that were definitely not coming from the TV.

Ruby furrowed her brow and leaned forward in bed to try to catch a glimpse out the bedroom door, which stood ajar. She debated getting up and seeing who it was, but she was all warm and cozy between the sheets. Besides, if they were people talking, Eli likely knew who they were and the conversation wouldn't last long. She didn't think it was rude to stay in bed at this hour, anyway.

She leaned back and tried to get back into *Misery*, but two thoughts kept nagging at her.

That voice didn't sound familiar.

I didn't hear the door open.

Sticking the bookmark between the pages, Ruby set the book back down on the nightstand and tossed the blankets aside. She wouldn't be able to relax until she figured out whose voice it was and what they wanted. Even if she embarrassed herself by going down in a bathrobe, it would help her—

She stopped moving when she heard a loud thud from downstairs. Almost as if someone fell or a stack of books were dropped.

Determined that she needed to investigate, Ruby set her feet on the hardwood and began to rise when she heard footsteps coming up the stairs.

Her heart raced and her mind ran through all of the possibilities—expanding due to her love of horror books, which now served as a new way to terrorize her. Building up the courage to scope things out anyway, she rose to her feet and took several tentative steps to the door.

You're being silly, Ruby, she told herself. *There's no one down there. It was probably just Eli making a mess.* She crept closer to the door and jumped when her husband's face suddenly appeared in the darkness. She let out a quick yelp.

Instantly, her heart rate slowed as the irrational panic subsided. A moment later, her face turned to confusion as the embarrassment for the thoughts she had only moments ago set in.

"What was that noise?" she asked quickly to disguise her paranoia.

"It was the phone." He stepped to his dresser and began to pull off his clothes.

"I didn't hear it ring." She stood with her hands on her hips, still too anxious to crawl back into bed. "And who was calling at this hour anyway?"

"Prank caller." He pulled his belt out of his jeans and set it on the top of the dresser. "I told them to stop calling."

"And that thud?" she asked.

"The phone slipped out of my hands." He pulled off his jeans and dug something out of one of the pockets. Rather than hang them on the knob to wear tomorrow, he balled them up and tossed them on the floor beside the dresser.

"If you're done wearing those, couldn't you at least put them in the hamper?"

Eli turned and stepped toward her quickly, slipping his hand around her and tossing her onto the bed. Startled, she looked up at him as he crawled on top of her and began kissing her hungrily. He moved down to her neck and she became overwhelmed by lust, before the nagging feeling that something wasn't right made her push him away.

"Hold on, Eli," she said. "Just wait." She crawled up a little higher on the bed to put distance between them. "Where is this coming from?"

"Can't I kiss my wife?" he asked. "Maybe a little more too?"

"But we just did it two days ago." That was one way she knew they were in a rut: sex came like clockwork every Sunday. As if it was something to check off on a to-do list.

"So?" he asked. "I want you now."

Ruby smiled at the spontaneity. Eli took it as an invitation to continue and he started working at her neck again, kissing it in that spot that she liked.

Her eyes fluttered open for a moment and she caught of glimpse of him fishing for something behind him. She tried to ask what he was doing, but his mouth pressed against hers kept her from saying anything.

The feeling that something wasn't right came flying back to her. Above her, Eli pulled a pocket knife out of the waistband of his underwear. As he flicked the blade open, her eyes widened in fear and she immediately pushed at his chest in an attempt to free herself, but the weight of him held her in place.

Eli reached for her throat with his free hand. In an instant, his face changed from seductive to sinister as he swatted away her feeble attempts to free herself from his grip. Instead, he removed his hand from her throat and used it to press one of her hands against her side.

She swatted at him with her free hand, squirming and thrashing on the bed. But the way she was restrained left most of her torso exposed.

The perfect opportunity to jab the pocket knife into her once, twice, three times.

Ruby let out a shriek as the knife skewered through her. Eli adjusted his hand so it covered her mouth to muffle her screams. He delivered several more jabs, this time directly to her stomach.

Blood seeped out of her wounds, staining the white linens and pooling beneath her body. Still she fought to push him away; the pain not setting in. Her mind was focused on one thing only: get away.

But with each movement she made, her heart pumped more blood out of her, killing her faster as the panic took over. With her strength diminished, her movements slowed to a stop and she finally succumbed to her wounds.

Eli stood, his own heart racing, and looked down at his work. Grinning, he turned and stepped to the bathroom for a shower.

CHAPTER 2

Don't forget to read Chapters Four and Five in your textbook," Professor Roger Mitchell said at the end of class. "And more importantly, finish reading the Edith Wharton book! We'll be discussing it on Friday, so please be prepared. Have a nice day everyone!"

Kathy sat at her seat and scribbled out the homework at the top of the page in her notebook. If she learned anything in her nearly two months of college, it was to take notes on everything, especially the homework.

She just didn't think there'd be this much *reading*.

With most of the rest of the class filing out faster than she thought humanly possible, Kathy stuffed her books back into her bag while her mind raced with everything she had to do.

The reading Roger just assigned would take her several hours. At least they were having a discussion on it and not a reflection essay. That added even more to her workload, which was already threatening to break her. The good thing was, she actually liked this Early American Literature class.

Her Spanish 101 class, on the other hand, made her tense up every time she even thought about it. Learning a foreign language never interested her, but it was one of the few entry-level classes left so close to the start of the semester—since she registered only two weeks before classes started—and both her advisor and Samantha said that getting the foreign language class out of the way early was a good plan.

Of course, neither of them had to do the actual work.

Hauling her heavy backpack up onto her shoulder, Kathy felt it smack into someone behind her when she got it on her back.

"Oh, I'm so sorry!" she said when she saw Harry, one of her classmates, recoil the arm she had hit.

"Do you have enough books in there?" He offered a perfect smile that revealed dimples on both sides of his cheeks.

Kathy noted how cute he was her first day, but there were several things holding her back from pursuing Harry. Chief among them was that she was here to learn, not find a boyfriend. If she started blurring that line with boys, she'd lose all focus.

"Sorry," she said. "Would you believe I'm only taking two

classes?" She pointed to the door. "Mind if we walk and talk? I have to get to work soon."

Harry stood back and held out his arm for Kathy to go first. She maneuvered out between the tight row of tables and into the hallway, which very much resembled a barn.

Porreco College was fairly new, having been a farmstead prior to its first classes only the previous year. Despite it's suburban location, there was no denying that the school still had remnants of its more rural past. Namely, the two silos that stood high above all the other buildings on the property.

It made for a quirky anecdote and a notable landmark to look for the few times Kathy drove.

"So I was wondering if you'd like to study together sometime," Harry said.

"For this class? I mean, it's just a bunch of reading, mostly. And I'm already kind of a slow reader and this stuff isn't exactly a *light* read."

He chuckled and pushed open the door at the end of the hallway that led out to the sidewalk. He held it back for Kathy to step through. "Okay, so maybe disguising my intent as *studying* was a bad idea. How about a drink, then?"

"A drink?" she asked, then blurted, "Are you even old enough to drink?"

That was another downside to her starting classes. She was twenty-one taking freshmen classes while most of her classmates were still only eighteen, having started college right after high school. Like most people did. She didn't think three years would make that big of a difference, but in many of the discussions they had had in class about the reading, she usually felt so *old*. Of course, with what she and Samantha dealt with as witches, Kathy knew she was more mature than most twenty-one-year-olds.

Harry laughed again. "Okay, so we can't *go out* for a drink, but if you're cool with it, we could hang in my parents' garage. They won't care."

Kathy pulled the sleeves down on her sweater as they made it out to the parking lot, where the occasional gust of wind brought a chill to the otherwise sunny day.

"As tempting as indulging in underage drinking is, I think I'm going to have to pass," she said. "I just have a lot going on right now with this class and work and my sister's getting married soon."

"You still haven't mentioned a boyfriend," he pushed with a smirk. "Are you seeing anyone?"

Immediately, Kathy's mind went to Milo. While what they had was nothing official, the two of them had been getting together at least once a week for the last couple of months. Surprisingly, their encounters were in the daylight, even though they met at a nightclub. In her experience, guys she met in the wee hours of the night never quite looked—or acted—the same once she got them in the light and introduced them to her life with responsibilities.

Not that she usually had a ton of responsibilities, other than magical ones.

"Um…sort of," she said to Harry. Milo certainly wasn't her boyfriend, but it would be a bit of a slap in the face to him if she suddenly started seeing someone else too. As far as she knew, Milo wasn't even talking to any other girls. He had a lot going on too.

"So is that a maybe?"

Kathy glanced at her watch. "I have to get to the bus stop if I'm going to make it to work on time, I should—"

"I could drive you."

And show him that she worked at the mall, thus proving that she wasn't as sophisticated as she just made herself sound? Pass.

"That's really sweet of you, but I don't want to burden you. I think I'm going to stick with the bus." She started walking backward across the parking lot to the bus stop on W 38th Street.

"It's no burden!" Harry called out as she put more distance between them.

She pretended she didn't hear and waved. "We'll talk Friday at our next class!"

"Wait, Kathy!"

She let out a heavy sigh and stopped moving, their conversation even more awkward now that there was nearly ten feet between them.

"I was hoping to invite you to a Halloween party this

weekend," he admitted.

Halloween was Monday, but all the parties were this weekend. With everything going on, Kathy had nearly forgotten about the holiday, which was almost like a witch sin.

"It's at a friend of mine's house," he went on. "We don't need to call it a date or anything like that, but I'd like to see more of you. Outside of class."

Kathy stammered and looked back to the bus stop. The next bus would arrive soon and she really didn't want to run with her heavy backpack. That would make standing at work for the next eight hours even more dreadful.

"I have to go," she said. "I'm sorry! We'll talk Friday!" Turning, she walked toward the bus stop faster than she usually did, cursing herself the whole way for making the entirety of that conversation with Harry uncomfortably awkward.

CHAPTER 3

Samantha shut the door to her car and slung her bag over her shoulder when she got home. It had been a long day. She walked down to the sidewalk and took in the large mature trees whose leaves had turned to beautiful warm fall colors. It was about the only bit of reprieve she'd have all day. She had a million things to do at work and the last thing she needed was the headache of her future mother-in-law coming to her house for the first time to plan the wedding.

Or rather, *take over* planning the wedding.

The whole way home, Samantha had been forming rebuttals to snide comments she assumed Steven's mother would make. And yet those comebacks would probably only venture as far as the tip of her tongue.

Across the street, Eli Harding carried the back half of a recliner down his driveway. The bottom half of the chair sat at the curb. When he dropped the pieces together, he smiled and waved at Samantha.

"Hi Eli," she called out to him. "How's the new place?" Eli and his wife, Ruby, were clients of her firm. They were roughly the same age as Samantha and she loved the idea that another young couple had moved onto the street.

Eli crossed over to her side and stood at the curb beside Samantha. "Still needs some work, but we're excited to get our hands dirty. Ruby's got all kinds of ideas for projects from those home magazines." He rolled his eyes and smiled. "Whatever makes her happy."

"'Happy wife, happy life' has a grain of truth to it," she admitted.

He laughed. "Hey, you're about to find that out for yourself, aren't you? Big day's coming up."

"Not for a couple more months," Samantha said. "Actually, Steven and his mother are supposed to be over today to work on some more plans, so I should probably—"

"Do you have a lot to work on?"

She shrugged. "I guess. Kathy and I picked out a couple dresses a few weeks ago. Still haven't pulled the trigger on any one in particular."

"Isn't that usually the first thing you do?"

"I'm not too picky about it. Honestly, I'm only going to wear it one day, so the better deal I get on it the happier I'll be. And I got a pretty good deal."

"Geez, I think I married the wrong woman." He laughed.

Samantha rolled her eyes. "Don't say that! Ruby's great."

"Of course, yeah. I love her. She's definitely the one for me and all that, but sometimes I just wish she'd be able to cut back on her spending, you know?"

She furrowed her brow, thinking back to their tax returns. From what she remembered, Eli was the one who spent more money than Ruby did. But then, Samantha saw a lot of files come across her desk. She could've just been remembering wrong.

The two neighbors both turned when Steven pulled into the driveway behind Samantha's car. They watched as he got out and trotted over to them.

"Sorry, had a hard time getting out of the office," he said. Turning to Eli, he thrust out his hand. "Hi, I'm Steven, Samantha's fiancé."

Eli greeted him, but looked to Samantha. "Oh, so this is Mr. Right? Well, I'll make sure to stand out of your way." He laughed and patted Steven hard on the shoulder. "Geez, do you live at the gym?"

Steven laughed along politely as Samantha looked her fiancé up and down. Steven looked good, but he was by no means a hugely muscular guy. Her eyes went up to Steven's face and saw just how uncomfortable he looked.

"Eli and his wife, Ruby, are some of my clients." Samantha pointed across the street. "They just moved in right over there."

"Oh okay." Steven nodded to the recliner at the curb. "You're not throwing that chair away, are you? Looks comfortable."

Eli waved it off. "Nah, it's got a big tear in the back. Damaged in the move, you know?"

"I've had that happen," Steven said. "As if you don't spend enough money when you move, right?"

"I know!" he said with his eyebrows raised. "I mean, it's completely out of control. First you try to get rid of all your stuff so there's extra garbage fees and that kind of thing. Then you have to shell out all this money for a moving truck and some people to help you get all your furniture out of your old place and into your new one. Then you have to buy more furniture and curtains and linens and oh my God, it just doesn't stop!"

"Well, hey, next time you need help moving, just let me know," Steven offered.

Eli burst out laughing and patted Steven on the arm again. "This guy! Kicking me out of the neighborhood already!"

"No, that's not—"

"I'm just teasing, I'm just teasing." He waved his hand at Steven to quiet him. "No, I appreciate your confidence. Offering your help *after* the work's done."

This time, Steven remained quiet, his face flaring red once more. Samantha could tell he didn't know what to say.

From beside him, she smiled politely. "Well, it was nice

talking to you, Eli. But we need to get ready for when Steven's mom comes later."

"Oh sure," Eli said. "You've got a lot of work to do! Hey, before you go, I just wanted to invite you guys to a little Halloween party Ruby and I are having on Saturday. I know it's a few days early, what with Halloween being on Monday and all, but we figured more people would come this way."

Samantha and Steven exchanged looks, wordlessly trying to negotiate a reason why they couldn't come. Finally, Samantha gave in to the inevitable.

"Sure, sounds fun."

"Yeah, it'll be a blast," Eli said. "Think of it as a housewarming party of sorts—but no gifts! We're doing this to meet the neighbors. We're not trying to hold our hand out or anything like that."

"Of course not," Steven said.

"Invite anyone you want," Eli went on. "Your sister—Kathy, is it?"

Samantha nodded.

"She's welcome, even her gentleman friend if she's got one. Bring them all!"

"She's always got a gentleman friend," Steven said with a grin.

Samantha smacked his arm as a warning. "I'll let her know."

"The more the merrier!" Eli said. "Hey, it was nice talking to you. You two take it easy now, okay? I'll see you later!" He offered another wave and then jogged across the street and back to his house.

Steven looked at Samantha. "He's…"

"I know. But we can go to the party and play nice. With them living across the street, he's obviously not going anywhere."

He glanced back at Eli's house. "Unfortunately."

"I'm more concerned about your mother coming over and taking over the wedding." Samantha jabbed her finger into his chest playfully. "That means you and I have some decisions to make before she gets here. Let's go."

More by the Author

To find more books by the author, visit
DavidNethBooks.com/Books

* * *

Subscribe to his newsletter to be the first to know of new
releases and special deals!
DavidNethBooks.com/Newsletter

* * *

If you enjoyed the book, please consider leaving a review
on Goodreads or the retailer you bought it from. Reviews
help potential readers determine whether they'll enjoy a
book, so any comments on what you thought of the story
would be very helpful!

About the Author

David Neth is the author of the Coven series, the Under the Moon series, Heat series, the Fuse series, and other stories. He lives in Batavia, NY, where he dreams of a successful publishing career and opening his own bookstore.

Also writes small town romance as D. Allen.

www.DavidNethBooks.com

www.facebook.com/DavidNethBooks